T0094557

MORDECHAI SCHAMZ

Marc Cholodenko

Translated by Dominic Di Bernardi

Dalkey Archive Press

Originally published by Hachette as *Mordechai Schamz* (*Loin de Dieu II*), 1982
Copyright © 1982 by Hachette
Translation copyright © 1988 by Dominic Di Bernardi
English language copyright © 1988 by Dalkey Archive Press
First U.S. edition, 1988
First paperback edition, 2000
All rights reserved

Library of Congress Cataloging-in-Publication Data:

Cholodenko, Marc, 1950-
     [Mordechai Schamz. English]
     Mordechai Schamz / Marc Cholodenko ; translated by Dominic Di Bernardi.
          p. cm.
     ISBN 1-56478-246-8 (alk. paper)
     I. Di Bernardi, Dominic. II. Title.

PQ2663.H575 M6713 2000
843'.914—dc21   00-020969

Partially funded by grants from the French Ministry of Culture, the National Endowment for the Arts, a federal agency, and the Illinois Arts Council, a state agency.

Dalkey Archive Press
www.dalkeyarchive.com

Printed on permanent/durable acid-free paper and bound in the United States of America.

for Sri Chinmoy

Mordechai Schamz went to the swimming pool last summer. Upon sighting those practically naked bodies by the waters, he took to thinking—no, it wasn't actually a thought, but rather a feeling, a sensation, more precisely. The sensation took hold of him that this spectacle was not for him. What is a spectacle? he said to himself, what is this something that is given us to see if not an offering, a present, a promise, yes, the possibility of a possession? Concerning this possession, its manner, no doubt, could never be made precise to our mind, and yet this imprecision subtracts nothing from the subtle reality our feeling confers upon it. Perhaps because the possibility is what counts more than the possession. And from what is possible, obviously, nothing can be subtracted. And this question of possibility is precisely what I refuse. Or rather I see it refused myself, by myself—that is more exact. Even so I would need to know what this possibility is. How could I find this out? What to choose, within this spectacle, that could become the object of an eventual possession? Must I, in the end, choose: is not the totality what is offered me? No doubt: here is the water, here the bodies, their nakedness, but also what is concealed from me, the faces, the beautiful blue sky, the boards, the bathing huts (oh oh—the huts), and from the unified whole, myself not being allowed to disregard or to distinguish any feature, something manifests itself to my mind, which my mind refuses to recognize and does not want to admit. Is it a single word? Several words of a single sentence? An entire sentence? A speech? Or something else entirely? What is the point, however, of this interrogation since I refuse to answer? All that I will know and all that I want to know is that from this refusal I draw the day's happiness. Yes, here is a day most calm and most cheerful. A most lovely day. And, breaking off there, Mordechai Schamz went bathing.

Such a gaze he has, this Mordechai Schamz! Such a gaze! He's a sorcerer. He deserves neither praise nor blame: as you know, this is the way it is with all sorcerers. The instant his gaze falls upon you, you find yourself clothed in loose-fitting, solemn but nonetheless plain garments. You sense that, if you were to make the slightest move, the clothes would behave exactly like water at night in this atmosphere steeped in secrecy, and create brief shimmers of light. You alone are important in the heart of a new world where you are held by Mordechai Schamz's gaze. Nevertheless, the impression has faded, and now you could not really explain what was so peculiar about those eyes. The man himself, as a matter of fact, does not strike you as special in any way. What he has that's exceptional he holds fast around himself, like a swarm of very tiny birds that otherwise might risk escaping. This must explain the gaze: he lowered his guard for a very brief instant and let it escape. He is a man like any other; you were simply distracted for a moment and, what's more, his eyes are not even large. There's nothing about him that sets him apart from the hundreds of people you objectively see every day. As for the subjective experience, perhaps he leaves behind, briefly, the regret of not having taken him by the shoulders so you could tender your eyes once again to his gaze and assure yourself that it really didn't happen. This experience of being present face to face with him in a place other than where you found yourself. But, as for the feelings a man inspires, each one of us can say everything, and even invent everything, with no risk of incurring any sanction from reality since in such a matter objectivity cannot be said to exist.

Quite recently, Mordechai Schamz bore witness to an accident—more precisely to its immediate aftermath. In all likelihood, it had only just occurred when he passed in the vicinity of the scene. He did not stop. Who does not have, at these moments, the idea of putting himself in the victim's place, simultaneously with a thought of gratitude for the providence that has spared us, yet once again, such a fate? Thus it was, of course, for Mordechai Schamz. Then, persevering in this direction, he wondered what would become of him if he found himself in the place of the person he had just come across. But no answer could be hoped for. It was but possible to vaguely dream of such an eventuality. All told, he continued, such is the way we live each passing moment— and the process is so habitual that a bit of blood is needed at the very least to make it remarkable for us. Our world consists only of glances we have of its periphery, with no hope of ever seeing anything but what we are able to imagine. It is empty, and consists only of our dream of what the surrounding worlds are. Absent to itself, it is composed exclusively of the equal absence of the worlds it verges on. Quite like a road: a road exists only by virtue of the space it displaces, traverses, and continues through unawares. Whether it go on, madly seeking to pierce its neighboring secrets by every conceivable detour, turn, and zigzag, it would not to any less a degree continue to be the very thing that pierces and traverses in ignorance. In conclusion, he concludes, one hardly is, and the little that one is, consists of what one is not. Thus Mordechai Schamz went on, continuing along his path, for he could not do otherwise, all the while saying to himself that what he had so hastily thought (this is the only way he can think—with the idea that his thought is something real, existing as an object, and whose nature is to flee him) had perhaps been distorted by the very haste which had conceived it.

A memory from the early childhood of Mordechai Schamz. Do you remember the poodle Dagobert, Mordechai? A large, very elegant beast, always impeccably groomed, lion-style. What have you learned since you knew that expression? Anyway: it is wintertime—autumn's final days; a pond bordered with trees at dusk, under a sky that had been uniformly leaden all day long; he no longer knows how far from the water, leading he doesn't know quite where, a stairway, very wide and very short, a single flight but whose steps, long and low as they are, seem to the little man as so many landings. He had climbed a few when the incident took place, in connection with the dog. He never found out if this connection was one of causality or simultaneity. This he knows, and he remembers in the language of his boyhood: there is the dog and he falls. His parents told him that he had fainted. As for him, he only remembers the tumble on the stairs, before the water, under the sky, with the dog. He even recalls the smell of the dog, unless it be the scene's itself. Therein are found the numberless components of the incident, all compressed in the memory of this smell, and which he will never be able to separate from each other, isolate in words, sentences, thoughts. It's a great loss, for the incident had its importance, and its importance was held in its components, and its components are now found in a place that is not within his intellectual power to attain, ignorant as he is of the space comprising it. A loss, no doubt, but of what? Mordechai Schamz says to himself. It is in this way, in the end, that all things remain with us that were important: through memory, emptied of what they were, of the fact they were important.

While Mordechai Schamz was walking along in the street, this sentence came to his mind: When my heart opens, it's like a stone splitting apart. It surprised him, since he could not attach it to any of his preceding thoughts and, especially, because it was based on nothing. Had he ever actually felt his heart open? Well, no—even less so this stone splitting apart. Yet it seemed to have imposed itself upon him as an obvious fact, the pure truth. *The pure truth*—a striking expression: perhaps, after all, the truth must never have been in contact with experience for it to reach us utterly pure, and present itself intact to our eyes. The more he sought to discover in his past an experience that might render it objective and the more this search appeared vain, the more, in an opposite way, was strengthened within him the feeling of the obvious fact inspired by this affirmation that seemed to have been made by itself. In the end, why not accept it as an element of information provided by an authority, of which he had not the least proof that it might not be as infallible, or even more so, than that of his own consciousness? Thus he did, and polished the formulation in the following manner: When the heart of Mordechai Schamz opens, it is like a stone splitting apart; this stone having grown hard not only through all the pain undergone by those which it made to suffer but furthermore by all the pain it has spared itself (if one grants that a heart which has already suffered its share, by opening, must leave place equally large for all the happiness it can conceive, to all the pain that others have borne in its place), then, once estimated the exceptional density of the matter needed to be dissociated, an idea can be formed of the force necessary to open Mordechai Schamz's heart. Despite everything, he had no clear idea of what that meant—along with the feeling of having somewhat exaggerated.

Observant and sensitive as he is, Mordechai Schamz was born to be a poet. But if the Muse, until now, has not offered herself to him, it is because he has never opened his arms to her. About her, nevertheless, as about the effects her company had upon others, he knows far more than those who fancy themselves in her favor. Obviously, not the slightest envy nor contempt; that's not Mordechai Schamz's style— and then, is he not far more the poet than they, a poet of life? It is a statement of fact for whomever has seen him, if only for a brief instant. Everything in his look and his ways proclaims it: Mordechai Schamz is a bird and what to a bird are the branches of trees, the state of the air and the prodigality of the fields, such to him is life itself. The matter requires an explanation, and yet how to provide it? Is Mordechai Schamz a bird because, like a bird's, his gaze never seems to settle or because he seems not to have any attachments or because he seems not to have any feelings or because he seems always on the point of leaving? To affirm one or the other of these things would be only to explain appearance by means of appearance, one comparison by another. But what an explanation cannot provide, perhaps an example will. Thinking one day about poetry and about what held him back from composing some, Mordechai Schamz said to himself: would it not be a good thing to live only on charity! To expect everything from someone other than oneself! Not only for drink, for food, and for lodging but equally for sight, touch, smell, thought, sleep, dream and even giving! And this thought for a long while placed him in a great state of exaltation. Of course these thoughts, this state, ephemeral as they were, could equally well be considered as appearances; but what we know of the bird is also appearance.

Yes, on occasion, but *only* in his thoughts, Mordechai Schamz is *virtually* mad. Now those are two rather restrictive adverbs. Are they present to signify that he is no more mad than the majority of people? Perhaps and perhaps not. Come on now! The joke has gone on long enough; a decision must be reached—some examples, some facts. Here is one: it happens to him that he does not feel he is a man—does not feel he is fit to be a man. Yes. Where would I be today, he says to himself, if man had invented, for his children, the proof concerning the eagle that Brunetto Latini describes thus: "And whereupon an eagle begets its offspring, it holds them in its claw directly to the sun's rays, and those that look directly without flinching are retained and nourished as worthy, and those whose eyes flinch are rejected and thrown from the nest, as bastards, not through cruelty of nature, but through rectitude of judgment; for the eagle does not hunt them as its offspring, but as alien creatures." No doubt if being cast down had not befallen me, I would be better off than I am today. I would have found my place. But what can be the place of a man who seems to be a man and is not so?

And, furthermore, does not know in what respect he is not so? What place does man make for those of his fellow creatures whom he rejects? Aside from the insane asylum and the prison, I see no other. Would I be comfortable there? That I would know only if I were there. But what would best suit me, I think, would be to be a man—for I am, in a definite way although not known by me—without a number. Neither beside nor above nor below, but simply not counted—an oversight in the great account of mankind. Whatever I may say or do, nothing that would issue from me would be counted. But who knows, Mordechai Schamz suddenly asks himself, if through some extraordinary favor this is not already the way things are?

Here is what led Mordechai Schamz to institute the practice of his celebrated monologues. If the reality of the things concerning us, members of the human race, he mused one day, is often conceived in the silence of thought, it is nonetheless irrefutable that this reality is only brought to completion in the sound of the linguistic utterance, as is proved by the evidence of these famous, exemplary, and extreme expressions: I love you—fire!—I don't love you—cease fire, etc. And if what is expressed is not always what is signified (thus "The weather's nice" may mean "I love you," "let's go," "fire") nor what is signified is recognized by the person who is signifying (the man expressing his opinion about the weather can be unaware that he is declaring his love), nevertheless the thing will have been, whether you like it or not, duly inscribed in the large, eternal, and exhaustive register of reality. Therefore, it is not a good thing that I remain silent, but on the contrary every day I must ensure the production of a few completed realities by means of one or more verbal exteriorizations. And this is why, since that time, Mordechai Schamz has not let a day go by without piercing his silence with a few remarks. Their content is of no importance to him. All that is important is that they hold fast around themselves, as the barnacle on a plank, as the mother-of-pearl with a grain of sand, a part of what ceaselessly moves about and passes by within the sounding secret of this tacit being. In this both modest and scrupulous manner, Mordechai Schamz does not despair that one day far into the future, or not all that far, within the span of time which will have been allotted him, and after having said almost nothing, that he may have expressed everything, perhaps. And then, since pleasure is what counts most in this life, what delicious moments will have been spent dreaming about everything meaningful—such a frail skiff, this: "Oh, such a lovely tree," isolated upon the ocean of a long day— about everything that will have grown up around it, trailed after it, without taking into account what it carries in its flanks and draws close to its sides.

Mordechai Schamz's physical appearance. What's that, the fellow is wondering, that sort of big tramp? That big sort of tramp—that big and strange sort of bum. It's due to the fact that, without being particularly remarkable, at bottom, nor, to all appearances, filthy, the initial purpose of his clothes seems to have been perverted—even though this is not the case. Is it his silhouette, then, which seems to have been adapted, by a sort of compression, to the shape of his clothes? Whatever the case may be, and without being able to define its nature and origin, Mordechai Schamz's appearance inspires in the fellow a powerful impression of strangeness. And what if it was his gait? This might well be possible.

Indeed, although once again with nothing particularly out of the ordinary about it, it could be compared—and only compared—to a tired man's gait whom events oblige to simulate an almost youthful drive and animation, but it could just as well be the gait of a child assuming the airs of an adult. Now this is quite confusing. Perhaps he's a madman, you say to yourself; then you decide otherwise—you are even a little embarrassed about having contemplated such an easy solution. No, it's all expertly controlled, perfectly of a piece and in impeccable order. He's not a madman, nor a tramp; he's a normal man, yes, quite normal, at bottom, and even rather elegant—very elegant, in fact. That's the reason he seems so strange—no, *strange* is not the word; why he seems so *foreign,* perhaps. He is an elegant stranger who hails from a foreign country whose manners and customs are unfamiliar in our land—that's all. And what's more, you don't wish to ponder this matter any further; suddenly you have had enough of the attention you have brought to bear on this man. It has even angered you a little. *Disheartened* is the accurate word—even though you hide it from yourself. You have already seen him too much—you have had your fill of him. That's all: you have the impression that he has come out of a place you would not have liked to be—and you feel even less like following him where he is headed. However, this is not reason enough to make Mordechai Schamz unlikeable.

From Mordechai S. to Olympe T.

Dearest,

It is most genuinely, as you know, that I hope you are well

and that your return letter will so inform me. As for myself, since you show the exquisite kindness to concern yourself with such a matter, there is my torment, habitual but, as you do not fail to suspect (forgive the verb, which so poorly suits your nature but which aptly translates the feelings I wish to inspire in my regard), also fictive. Is it not worse, horribly worse? Why ask myself and ask you a question to which we both know the answer? It is a little like masturbation (excuse me for evoking such a practice to such a young girl but I can conceive of no other comparison and it is the privilege of your age—discounting your exceptional intelligence and sensibility—to know nothing and to understand everything, far more exactly than those who know) in relation to the sexual act: the result is the same but one is (I am now speaking only about the pain, of course) deprived of reality's compensations which are—my God, I don't know—which are perhaps that one feels oneself participating in a sort of community of truth, and through that in a state of mutuality with the rest of mankind which, so I feel, ought to in a sense mitigate my ignorance of how harsh the sorrow is—somewhat, if you will, and very roughly speaking, like knowing you are not the only person locked up in a prison. So much for me, my good, good friend, and my deliriums. Forgive me, forgive me for inflicting them upon you, but you know it would relieve me even if I could be (which also means that in a certain way, no doubt mysterious, I ought to be relieved all the same). And then you know full well that a person only wearies those he loves—which provides you the measure of my love, does it not? Quickly, quickly, a word about you, about how well things are, and about your dear family.

Your Mordechai

Often, very often, Mordechai Schamz looks at the sky. What does he see there? He sees himself there, asking himself what he sees there. Then: might there be but this, everywhere in the abundance of what offers itself to our eyes—but this: the reflection of what he interrogates there? But this! he exclaims inwardly, suddenly ashamed about having expressed the qualification. Is this not enough? Is this not everything? But I have expressed myself poorly. I ought to have said either *the reflection of his interrogation* or *what he interrogates there* and not *the reflection of what he interrogates there,* for what he would then interrogate would not be in what he sees but within himself. Unless I may have expressed myself correctly without knowing it. Is such a thing truly possible, to express the truth without knowing it and afterward to catch up with it in the nick of time, at the very moment when you were going to continue on without seeing it? But what can you do with interrogations, if not pile them up ceaselessly one atop the other? he interrogates himself one last time, his head still thrown back skyward, his neck aching, and the object of curiosity of passersby. Let them be brushed aside, and your eyes turn resolutely from this useless pile, and then you can consider with a confident gaze and joy in your heart the new weightless task offering itself to our desire for action: the pile of affirmations to be raised. Of course, if the difference between them hinges only upon a point of grammar, no point in contemplating going very far, any farther than, for example: in the sky I look at the reflection of what I interrogate there. But if the affirmation is considered as one means, yes—one—means, he goes on, more and more slowly, in exact step with his thought which slows and brightens, until it becomes diaphanous, yes, one means—to go—to go farther—farther than the affirmed thing itself (for he has regained, and his thought with him, thickness and celerity), that is to say if it is considered, on the contrary, as one thing in itself, without an object—one, yes, of all things. But the thought stopped, so diaphanous that it attains the very transparency offered to Mordechai Schamz's gaze by a perfectly affirmative sky.

Life hangs upon Mordechai Schamz. She clings to him, adores him. She is his tempestuous mistress. Oh no, there is not a thing he might do that she would not worship to the point of being jealous of his slightest gestures. She is jealous, yes: like a lioness. Here, come, closer, stay a little closer, she seems, every second, to charge and entreat him. It is this intimate blend of order and prayer which characterizes her relationship to him. Quite obviously, she also holds several advantages. She more than he? A delicate question concerning a delicate balance. In the end, it is, as with everything, rather a question of point of view. If you look from life's, you clearly see Mordechai Schamz elusive, dancing, monolithic, relentless: an odd spouse, as it were. But if his own gaze is assumed, you can see in what respect she can feel herself paid back, white as she is, svelte, very proud, barely adorned. Only the allegory, practical and even justifiable, in the stranger's hands, sees her power reduced to nothing, and her legitimacy largely damaged once she finds herself placed in the grasp of one or several subjects. Thus, let her disappear, with the person who handled her, and may they remain alone, one to one, he seated on one of his dear benches in one of his dear gardens, she in the place depending on the locations and times crisscrossing all around and passing through, and look now how the order of values rigidifies and is less discernible, reducing idle chatter to subtleties too close to what is impalpable or to the crude mode of useless enumeration. Once the limpidity of the air and the gaze of a faraway child are brushed aside on the one hand, and on the other the number of trees, chairs and passersby, only then may Mordechai Schamz be heard murmuring a few words that he himself would not hear, that would perhaps permit something to be arranged, provided all the same a promise is made not to recall them to yourself, that is to say, that you hear them as if you did not hear them.

Mordechai Schamz would like to invent something. He has been thinking about it for a while and has long since set his mind to it: I am going to invent something. He is experiencing both the necessity and the difficulty. Indeed, he senses that it ought to be a machine but he has no more technical understanding than he has of how it ought to operate. The machine already has a name: the Schamzette. He finds it quite charming: full of sweetness and humility— light and cheerful. No sooner does he utter it than it's as if it was speaking to him: "Hello, I'm the Schamzette, the joy of children, the solace of the old, a dependable friend and faithful servant to all those of both sexes who are between the two." Undoubtedly within this delicious name the machine is already full-blown, amusing and practical, dependable and universal. Now all that needs be done is to expose the particulars that this generalization conceals. But the important work is over. The machine exists; its name proves it. All that remains is to discover the place where it is hidden and, after all, as far as that goes, there's no hurry. Aren't lying in wait and tracking down the most amusing parts of the hunt? However, Mordechai Schamz does not deem his invention to be wild game. What's more, he feels he possesses even less rights over it than a hunter over his prey —has enough been said? No, he sees the machine as a friend, a female friend, hidden but indestructible, and who will reveal herself only at the very moment she knows is the best. He is surprised to find himself the object of such sweet solicitude. What has he done to deserve this? Perhaps it's not a question of what is deserved in such cases but rather that it has been so written since time immemorial that he, and he alone, would be the discoverer of the Schamzette, even if it means this latter remain sealed forever within the limbo of potential being in the event he would not have existed. The fact it bears his name is already more than one indication. Unless he's the one bearing its name, less one syllable as a sign of his subjection to it? And why not? Often, what merely appears to be idle daydreaming and even drifting off is a pure premonition of destiny. And what could be more enviable than to be Schamz, M., harbinger, discoverer, servant of the Schamzette?

It is a fact that Mordechai Schamz experiences the greatest reluctance to consume the goods of this world. Not that he has no desire to—no, the desire is not what is lacking and sometimes he even succumbs to it. Be that as it may, he feels himself unworthy to divert for his own use a part—however minuscule—of the great and radiant flood of merchandise whose course is fed and controlled by his fellow creatures who find themselves on its banks. Has not Mordechai Schamz unmasked his secret reasons in this simple descriptive statement? Under the pretext of illustrating the phenomenon of commerce with an image, has he not just mistaken the mass of his fellow creatures for that of a herd at the hour when thirst is quenched? In his eyes, does not coveting, appropriating, and slipping into a pair of trousers amount to voluntarily pouring yourself into the same mold as the billions of others who are liable to act likewise? To sum up, is it really unworthiness he experiences or disgust, which is quite the opposite? But no, this is all so stupid, he blurts out to himself. How can I have let myself be drawn into such a train of thought? To begin with, it's not a question of unworthiness. It's a question of uselessness. Because that's what I actually experience expending desire and will and money, when things could be otherwise. No, things cannot be otherwise. My desire would be for my situation to resemble the lily of the valley—that providence provide me with all I need. But isn't this once again to set myself beside other men? Because if everyone did as I would like to do, if no one busied himself with securing a pair of trousers, who would make and who would sell the indispensable object? Ah, thought is quite ferocious, forcing us to follow it through logically in order to complete it. But also, once again, I display my great pride, and most of all my great vanity, notes Mordechai Schamz, by dedicating all my energy to this search for some grand thought which can harbor my reluctance to purchase a pair of trousers.

Things that are said to Mordechai Schamz. To reckon that, according to the popular expression, "it goes in one ear and out the other," would be sorely mistaken—it is quite the opposite; and it comes to the same thing. The matter appears complicated but it is very simple. As for what is said to him, Mordechai Schamz listens not only attentively but gratefully. Indeed it strikes him that only compassion can explain the fact a person desires to address himself to someone who matters so little as he; thus does he hear only the speech directed at him as a pretext for the expression of the utterly disinterested feeling that his insignificance has awakened.

And what weight to give to this pretext? But this weight, however so light, with which the curtain of words presses down, he still seeks to raise it so as to discover, upon the inward scene of his interlocutor, in all the glory of its purity, the compassion speaking through his mouth. So, it might be said without error that Mordechai Schamz does not listen to what is said to him but that he looks at what is signified to him. And if glasses existed to perceive, through appearance, reality, it might be possible, provided with them, to admire, behind the man facing the man speaking to him, Mordechai Schamz on his knees adoring the figure of charity. She has her arms outstretched toward him. She does not speak. She looks at him. And in this gaze, precise to the point that he pierces it, and so vast that he feels he is lost within it, he sees himself exist as himself, infinitely more complete than he will ever know himself, and also as the mass of all mankind. To see that, if such a thing were possible, would be to understand why the few people who address Mordechai Schamz remember they have spoken to him for a long time afterward. Perhaps some retain the impression of finding themselves before a listener too attentive to be sincere—in a certain respect they are right, and are mistaken to the same extent.

Mordechai Schamz almost never remembers his dreams. Perhaps the reason is he pays them such scant attention. He considers that, all told, he has no special reason to attach much importance to what he was when he was prone and asleep during those moments he finds himself up and awake. Does the dreamer set much store by the man he will be once the dream ends? In the end, he knows nothing about it. Perhaps he is the one who prepares us for what we will be once he no longer exists, in the same way that we prepare him, during the daytime, for what he will be at night. For after all here is a man who, awake, deems himself slumbering without this other in any way capable of retorting and the same would be the case in opposite circumstances: he would be deemed awake by his slumbering self without being able to do any more in his defense than the sleeper has. Where would justice lie in this instance, and where responsibility? Here is a dreamer who gives birth to a man awake who in turn conceives a dreamer and so on into infinity so that the responsibility for our being always finds itself behind us, in the one who has just passed. And does not the same apply to life? Indeed, if the past can be assimilated to a dream: the reality landing under our steps, pulverized— with no more existence than if it had been dreamed—what we ready ourselves to do in the very arriving instant, and what we conceive in the instant which is, and will be, reality and the present, finding itself between the two, such a reality then should be something like a movement or a thought that a man would have in his dream, and which, in the coming instant, would awaken him. Thus I would never be either dreaming or awake but always awakening within a dream which would be of myself awakening. This line of reasoning, Mordechai Schamz says to himself, no doubt, is arbitrary and forced and yet the image it culminates in, of this man who eternally stretches from one world to the other without ever being in either, possesses an indescribable air of truth.

Every man, remarks Mordechai Schamz, is entitled to the utmost pride as much as he is duty-bound to the utmost humility. For he is alone in being himself, among the numerous mass of like creatures. And I—I, he continues in one of those clownish sobs, I do not feel that I am quite myself or quite like anything. Thus I do not recognize my right nor my obligation to these extreme feelings. Indubitably it is by being pulled and pushed by each, and oppositely, alternatively and simultaneously, that our great thinkers made progress, and I have no alternative but to recognize that the absence of these two motivating drives prevents me from ever acceding to the still unexplored regions—if there be any—of this planet that is ourselves. However, what does the lack of a tool mean to me, since I do not have at my disposition the appropriate terrain? What at first glance appears to be deficient is on the contrary suitable. For if the tool in my possession is average, equally average is the terrain given over to my power of investigation. Alone in being average amidst all my like creatures, I am equally alone in my ability to explore this unique particle of boundless mankind. Obviously the results of my research will only apply to myself—which significantly reduces their scope as well as their interest. But have I just not affirmed that I am the sole member of my species, thus manifesting the utmost conceivable pride and, what's more, the sole of my species to be average, thus evincing the greatest imaginable humility? Well, then, I will not have been long in returning to other men, Mordechai Schamz says to himself. The exact time I needed to trace a perfect loop, that is to say, for me to perceive that I went around in circles. This congruent equivalence of act and of consciousness is very troubling. Perhaps if I had not perceived it I would have gone straight ahead.

Mordechai Schamz—you had to see him when he was a child! What a shame that so few saw him back then, and that the majority do not even remember, not counting those who have already died. He was more than pleasant to see, more than handsome—worse than that. This impression, so strange, out of the ordinary, produced by his all-so-very-tiny person, resulted first from the fact that he was as communicative as he was reserved. Each show of attention on the part of this child was experienced by the one to whom it was addressed as a secret grace—secret because he savored the ever-so-manifest particularity which the child, for his part, did not seem to be conscious of. Bizarre, a person may have thought, if such an impression had been able to be mastered on the spot and given form; it seems this little creature is casting upon me a gaze that does not belong to him, which he is merely relaying. And in similar fashion, whenever he shut himself up, put aside this blunt manner common to all children, it was as if he were shutting the door to a world he had been merely guarding. Thus, by having to recognize—unconsciously no doubt—the insignificance of his function at the same time as the enormity of his power, sensitive souls conceived toward him an irritated astonishment that made them speak of his beauty in negative terms and of his truly regal manners with a condescension they could never have justified. But therein perhaps Mordechai Schamz was not essentially different from other children. Who has not had, at least once, upon observing them, the impression that they are following the course of their lives under eyes which are not ours, and that the authority they submit themselves to is merely the screen for the one they recognize, an agreed-upon pretext, in a certain manner, between itself and them? If it is not, all told, in the impression he produced upon adults that Mordechai Schamz differed from other children, this in no way subtracts from the veracity of the affirmation according to which he was different. Indeed the impression does not depend on the nature of the object but upon the subject's receiving it. Mordechai

Schamz was a child different from others, whether or not there be anyone to say exactly in what respect.

The streets have always struck Mordechai Schamz as very weird. Yes, yes—very weird. No doubt their function, their necessity, the obvious fact of their usefulness do not escape his understanding. However upon stripping them, in his thought, of their obligatory character, they don this air of weirdness. But what is a street that is no longer a space established between dwellings for vehicles and pedestrians to circulate? If worse comes to worse, their usefulness can be dismissed as a place of passage, but the dwellings bordering them can never be eliminated, for they are what make streets streets, and not lanes, roads, byways, footpaths, or any other route of communication. Well now, that's precisely what Mordechai Schamz cannot accept. He wants streets to be for themselves, and not for what delimits them. He feels this to be so. But it is not enough to want or to feel—it must also be proved. That is, to find what defines them without limiting them, the positive character specific to them alone. Can it then be said that a street is the place where the greatest number of people cross paths? No, a street's traffic, no matter how sizable, cannot be compared to a highway's; the people, no, not really—but their glances? That's it: a street is the place where the greatest number of glances cross each other. And not only lengthwise, but also in every possible and imaginable direction—and still more—the nature of the place, naturally, being taken into account (but there are people who account for nothing)—at every calculable speed and duration. Ah, really, Mordechai Schamz says to himself, a street is a marvelous thing; but weird, no—I don't see what there is so weird about it. It must be because I haven't yet put my finger on what I was looking for. Still my procedure was sensible: streets seem weird to me—I seek what is specific to them, for that is how streets must be weird but, finding their specific nature, I did not find their weirdness. No doubt the reason is not to be found in their specific nature. It is perhaps in their banality. Or even solely within myself. Might it then be streets find *me* weird?

From Mordechai S. to G.

My Adored One,

I have utterly abandoned the idea of writing to you as if I were answering letters you might well have sent me. The idea was rather ridiculous, was it not? My poor Love, if I were to have foot and fist bound behind the door to my heart, how would you even be able to speak to me? At times I only hear your sobs, which is when tears come to my eyes. Sublime moments of pain! I wish that they would last longer. But weakness is, above all else and primarily, inconstancy. Hardly have I understood this than I have already forgotten. Not that I seek, *you* know far better than I, pleasure or even happiness. No. But because I am simply a devotee of time, I allow it to carry me away. Idols have always hidden you from the eyes of those who do not want to see you. And I do believe my personal idol is time. Consequently, there is no value that ultimately I do not submit to it, my pain first of all, despite the knowledge it is my dearest belonging. If only you struck me once and for all! If only you showered me relentlessly with every possible evil! Then no doubt I surely would be obliged to remain in pain: time itself will then be full of pain and I will no longer be able to seek refuge in its passing.

But I am asking you to impose Law upon me when I know that you can give only Faith. What is in your power to do is the last thing I would ask. I implore from you only what I know is in my power to repulse. Within my power your own powerlessness lies. Your own power lies in the powerlessness that I do not want to devote to you. Yes, it would take very little for me to turn toward you on the side I should, but I present you with the armor plate when I ought to offer the underbelly. No doubt this is all a game, and I know you are the one who falls to your knees while turning your back. No doubt with a little patience it will all work out. Yet you dwell where knowledge and patience no longer have meaning. That is why all the words that are addressed to you, if they have any value, are meaningless in your eyes, whereas they have a meaning in the mind of those who speak to you but no value in the heart. I kiss your heart, which is the world, where I am and that I do not see.

Mordechai

To say that Mordechai Schamz has "no memory whatsoever" would be an exaggeration. Of course, he does not have "as much as everyone." But to say that he has very little would be equally mistaken. Indeed, to speak of his memory in terms of quantity would be to approach the subject in a wrongheaded way. On the other hand, neither can it be a question of the quality alone of this faculty, whose existence depends solely on what it preserves. If Mordechai Schamz had a precise, well-reasoned and well-founded idea about life, to which he would conform as he conducted it, it might be proposed that he selects the contents of his memory according to criteria drawn from his vision of things, which would explain in part why it is so poor in facts. Still, if there exists someone who has no idea what he is doing here, he surely is such a man. Perhaps herein, on the contrary, is where an explanation must be sought for this strange feature of his nature: how can someone, in all logic, with so few ideas about what he does, have more memory about what he has done? However, if Mordechai Schamz's memory is nevertheless comparable to everyone else's insofar as it possesses the same capacity, and consequently the same volume, it is because he does not exclusively remember what has existed. He remembers in equal measure what has not existed, which is not what might have existed, or what he would have wanted to exist either, or even what he would be able to dream existed, but very simply what has not existed. It would be rank injustice, indeed, Mordechai Schamz remarks, if what quite evidently I fail (as all men) to live in my future becomes also bereft in my past on the pretext that my present is blind. And then, if it be true that memory, more than preserving the past, helps us to envisage the future, does not the memory of those passed absences, which I have not known, prepare me for those in my existence to come, and which one day it may well be that I will have to perceive?

One day Mordechai Schamz saw an elderly man crossing the street. Though he had seen many other elderly men who crossed many other streets, even so this one immediately distinguished himself from all the others in his mind. He was, strictly speaking, just at the threshold of old age, and something in his look, his gait, and the so simple way his beret was set on his head, very strongly signified renunciation. Not an ancient, brutal renunciation but a renunciation that was labored and fully realized through time, hour by hour, practiced at every hour and consumed by every hour, patiently, proudly. The rigor, so modest as to be barely perceptible, of his gestures and his attire, the severity, perfect in its discretion, of his entire appearance, seemed to Mordechai Schamz to prevent and even to intentionally forbid imagining that a life might lie within, and in his eyes conjured the image of one of those animal cadavers hollowed out by insects but whose intact exterior retains a look of life—he could only conceive that behind such an appearance, the interior of this man was as clean, as purged, as emptied. But that signified nothing, for behind this appearance, there was, as in all men, a life, indubitably. No doubt there was a life behind this appearance, Mordechai Schamz continued (not the sort of man to allow himself to be flustered by the irrefutable character of any objections found contrary to his own thought), but is not this appearance precisely the very image, as is the task of all appearances to be, of what it protects? Thus such a life should be possible, even if I am unable to conceive of what it must be. He watched the man, on the verge of old age, who was soon going to disappear from his sight, holding in his thought the image, which could not be filled with any meaning, of a life emptied, purged, but which did not any less produce in him a feeling that might well have been called one of envy if admiration was not so powerfully predominant.

While he is watching the passing cloud, which decomposes and recomposes upon itself, and again decomposes, constantly, up in the high wind, Mordechai Schamz says to himself, thus lending form to the discomfort inhabiting him: Undoubtedly I am watching this particular cloud but why does it seem to me that I do not really see it? Constantly must I make an effort to keep my eyes attached to it. Or rather I must constantly reattach them for, no sooner settled, they detach themselves. And all this to go where? To arrive back at myself, who yet has dedicated himself to contemplating this cloud. Am I so imperiously important that I do not have it in my power to be detached from myself for a few wretched instants? Important I cannot say; imperiously, there is not one second which, the need arising, would fail to bring me another proof of it. What to do about this, if not to relentlessly redirect toward the relinquished object the interest that is constantly returning to its source? Redirect, have I said? But does not the interest itself rebound upon arriving and immediately head back toward its object? For to attempt to remain within myself I have known nothing more successful than to try to fix myself upon the cloud. Thus I become the pole of attraction of my interest, for apparently it is in its nature to be repelled by the object one wishes to fix it on rather than to be attracted by the object from which one attempts to keep it at a distance. More than a faculty, whose functioning could be said to resemble a crane-grab, it is a back and forth motion regulating our relationship to the world, and we act exactly as do animals deprived of sight which regulate their movements according to the velocity at which the waves they emit are returned by surrounding objects. That strikes me as a security system just as indispensable for us as for them, concludes Mordechai Schamz. Indeed, if my interest were not to come back to me upon touching the object it aims for, I would forget myself and no doubt like to melt into a cloud so beautiful, I would leap through the window and—but who will tell me that in such case I would not be able to fly?

Ah! Mordechai Schamz should be given a good slap. That would teach him quite a few things. Given a good slap often —every day, perhaps. Yes, every day he ought to be slapped, but not by just anybody, not by those who, in the street, with the looks of brutes, easily resort to violence, but rather by people who are calm and stable, even gentle, who are admirable, friendly, people he would admire and befriend. The blows attributed to fate would do nothing to humble his vain arrogance; on the contrary, they would harden it. What's needed for such pride are the blows of fellowmen, voluntary, regular, daily blows, nothing less. Maybe then he would learn at last what it is to be a man, among men and with men. These blows ought to signify their contempt and their rejection. However, it could just as well happen that they have the opposite effect. Could not Mordechai Schamz see in them an indubitable proof of their interest in him and even of their solicitude? He would be quite capable of this, and in one way, he would not be wrong. That several persons think about him every day, dedicate a few daily minutes to thrashing him, irrefutably indicates a concern they have about him and verges on the kind of treatment that eventually would risk confirming the morbid attention he pays to himself. No, the contempt should be displayed haphazardly and assume forms as savage as they are unexpected. After all, you can always expect the contempt of those you know, but if a worthy stranger stopped Mordechai Schamz in the street to spit in his face, now that would go a long way in sparking closer interest on his part in the shadowy facets of his personality. Is my vileness so apparent, he would be forced to ask himself, that it commands the indignation of a passerby? Be careful: now it's no longer even an ethical question, but rather one of simple safety. And that would be a good thing, for there are creatures, including Mordechai Schamz, who are happy to pass judgment on themselves and to keep their guilt hidden from the world, as if too precious, undoubtedly, to be shown, or too rare to be understood.

Can it be said of Mordechai Schamz that there is a particular look about his face? In a way yes, and in a way no. At first sight, it is not especially remarkable—but for the person who knows him, it becomes so. But could that not be said about each and every one? In his case, however, the phenomenon is more pronounced. When you see him for the second time, you hardly recognize him. How comes it that such beauty has not struck us? As a matter of fact, no—it is not beauty, nor ugliness, obviously, and not even a real originality. What is surprising, when you give it some thought, is that he seems to exist behind his face—not so as to hide there but, on the contrary, to manifest himself. For Mordechai Schamz, it can be said, is an open man, and rather playful. But his features, very expressive, seem to the spectator not to manifest the feelings they express to the same degree and in the same manner that he perceives them in himself. It is really as if he were expressing himself through his face as through a screen. This manner of composing with appearances is as striking as it is disconcerting. Indeed, the share of responsibility the interlocutor finds himself forced to abandon to his own power of interpretation is so great that he can never be sure of not being mistaken. What does this man signify behind his face, he asks himself; is it more or less than what I see and hear? Does he only say something— does he only show something? Perhaps now it is as if, behind this face, he were walking along, after nightfall, through a great forest, his gaze upon the stars and singing words of his own invention. Thus it can be said that, knowingly or not, Mordechai Schamz enjoins his spectator to entrust himself to his imagination. And it is a little as if this latter, gaze fixed upon the stars, were walking along, after nightfall, through a great forest, singing words of his making. Hence, perhaps, this impression that he possesses some inexpressible kind of beauty.

Mordechai Schamz thinks at times that he would really like to be on a theater stage. Not that he likes showing himself—quite the opposite would be the case. What would he do on a stage and how did this fancy come to him? He would find it rather difficult to say. The fancy exists nevertheless. Even though it is not strictly speaking a desire but rather the loving idea of an eventuality: if chance placed him alone on a stage before an audience and forced him to stay there the average length of a performance, well then—yes, what would he do there? Would he feel himself obliged to do something? Could he not simply sit down and watch those who are watching him? No doubt, but such would not be the way, obviously, that he would be able to occupy his audience's attention for very long. One among them might well have the fancy to take the place of such a sorry clown. And that is something he does not want on any account. If he is on stage, it is to stay there. The fact is that he did not ask for it, and no more than for the audience there looking at him, but they both must remain in their assigned places. However, if nothing requires him to justify his presence, he still needs to impose it. Once again the question arises as to the means of accomplishing this. As for being amusing, even distracting, or interesting, such are out of the question. He is here in order to keep them on their side of the footlights while he keeps on his; neither more nor less—and he does not, for that, need to lower himself or ridicule himself, for then he would no longer be what he is and the situation would have no reason to exist. It is his duty to be himself before them such as he would be if they were not before him. Thus he cannot even speak to them, and if he started into a monologue it would be in simulation. Likewise, gestures are forbidden him that he would not make alone at home, or in the street and, there or here, they are neither remarkable nor numerous. All that remains for Mordechai Schamz is to hold himself there, in the simplest, strongest way he is able, while hoping there will not be a joker, or a maniac, who will come and put an end to his show before the time allotted him has elapsed.

It so happens to Mordechai Schamz that he looks at himself at length in the mirror. What thoughts animate him is something he himself does not know. Perhaps he has none. But has such a thing ever been seen? Let us rather say that they are silent, or invisible, or silent and invisible. In what world are they located? And he, without any apparent thought, in what world is he located? They are perhaps located in the same world, both unconscious one of the other. Or perhaps, fixed as he is at this moment upon appearances, he alone is the one who is not conscious of them, whereas they have retained an awareness of him. What can they think of him, when he is not there to think upon them? Most likely, things that would surprise him. Or it may be all they do is look at him, exactly as he does. Like himself, they have stopped, and through him look at him. How do they see him; what do they see of him? The thoughts that have escaped you, whose gaze can no longer be forced, do they have the look of truth? And in such a case, what is this look? To think that you live with something inside yourself that thinks you, and to the thought of which you do not have access, now that's disconcerting. And it is all the more so to think that this something is looking at you and even at times, when the occasion crops up, through your own organs, when they have been abandoned to it for a certain while. Thus not only is Mordechai Schamz in ignorance of the thoughts animating him, but equally so of the gaze appraising him. But disconcerting situations are not made to disconcert him who is the hero of his own life, while at the same time a historian of his own history. On the contrary, he plunges into and persists in such situations, for it is in these and in no others that the occasion is found to manifest what the other has as its task to record. And if the hero was unable, obviously, to name at the time the quality he displayed, the historian, this moment once passed, will retain the tenacity by having confirmed that it is with relief he then murmurs, at last making use of a function which he is sure belongs to himself alone, to this reflection with the ever-distant gaze: Mordechai Schamz.

A greater boor than Mordechai Schamz has rarely been seen, nor anyone more delightful. Imagine that now! What new nonsense is being spun? A delightful boor, a boorish delight? The affirmation, truth told, is as indisputable as it is indefensible, insofar as he keeps company with few people, if not to say with almost no one, and on those rare occasions his behavior can in no way be qualified as extraordinary. Who therefore, and in view of what, is able then to authorize himself to judge him in these terms? Mordechai Schamz is in the dark about this; however, this is what he hears. He hears it? Now there's something new; he hears voices now? He would like it to be so; it would make the thing less complicated than it is; it is not, indeed, because he knows nothing of its foundation or its origin that he can permit himself to sweep aside this judgment. Judgment it is, and must be considered as such. It has not issued from nothingness, and if it concerns him it is because he must feel himself concerned by it. So he does, for there is no one who is more desirous, in everything, to mend his ways. The difficulty, of course, in the present case, is that he does not know where in himself the boorishness or the delightfulness lies. But what is difficult is not impossible, and Mordechai Schamz exerts himself with great energy to detect the presence of both one and the other. I could thus formulate the hypothesis, he reflects, that these two features of my behavior apply only to myself, for never have I in my life surprised myself in the act of either charming people or treating them harshly. And in what way might I charm myself? By way of my boorishness? Perhaps. No doubt I at times am not averse to treating myself harshly. And I have this way of secretly congratulating myself for it—well, that's my manner of charming myself. Thus it would be, and inversely so, with my delightfulness, which would so happen to be, oh how oftentimes, so charming to myself. It is in this sense that I would be able to understand that I am a delightful boor and a boorish delight, that by being a boor I am charming to myself, and by being delightful I am a boor to myself. Regardless, remarks Mordechai Schamz, this is merely an hypothesis, and a rather flimsy one at that.

Mordechai Schamz has always known how to maintain a happy medium. Great were the temptations however sometimes that he had to combat so as not to veer to one or the other side. But he conquered them all. Most likely if he was, or will ever be, proud, it was, and will be, about that. For there are very few men who know how to resist. And it is not among those whom history preserves in public memory, in any case, that he will be able to find any. To accomplish this kind of exploit, one thing is absolutely certain, that men like himself are needed, those whose history that no history will be ever able to touch; for, in essence, they are beyond its reach. To know whether it was destiny which, from the outset, gave them, along with the ability, the aspiration to raise themselves so high or whether they gradually forged themselves the character and means such an enterprise required, no man exists, here below, who can say—all the more so since there is no one who has any interest in doing so, beginning with these very men themselves. No, there never was and there never will be a history to keep a record of these conquerors who know nothing of themselves or, more exactly, who are loathe to recognize themselves. The thought suddenly arises and strikes Mordechai Schamz that the simplest thing is to count himself excluded from the category he has just defined. Ah! now that's quite something, he inwardly shouts, to recognize myself such as I am ipso facto deprives me of the right to be so. Yet, such a right cannot be taken away by just anything, from just anyone. Therefore I did not exclude myself from my category; I merely withdraw my right to consider myself as a member of it: mine is a rather exceptional state, and furthermore, not at all surprising. Now for some while, indeed, I have suspected that with me there exists a sort of contradiction between the knowledge of being and being knowing itself—a contradiction that seems to be a pure and simple relationship of exclusion, wherein to know what I am prevents me from recognizing myself as being what I am and inversely to be what I know excludes that I recognize myself as knowing what I am. Will the day come, Mordechai Schamz questions himself, when I will be able to be what I know and know what I am simultaneously, without my being handicapping my knowledge and vice versa? On that day, in any case, I will have ceased maintaining this happy medium wherein I can straddle one half of being and one half of knowledge, all told, quite comfortably.

From Mordechai S. to Olympe T.

My Poor Darling!

Yet another piece of paper to add to your file. You are going to become, in spite of yourself, more of a specialist in myself than I am! This partly in an attempt to win forgiveness, partly by way of a joke and mostly in order to be serious. For I believe first of all that a person never knows himself; second, that there are those sorts, of which I am one, who do not really seek to know themselves. Why then, you will next say to me, do you mercilessly cram me with a knowledge which you yourself have no occasion for? Well, it's because I pity myself more than I do you. No, seriously now: I believe, in all honesty, not only that you can know me better than I can but most of all that that it is more important that you know me than that I know myself. For that, you have the perfect right to ask for my reasons when I can only provide you with feelings. I have the feeling, very sharp and very definite, my good soul, my darling, my providential woman, that as much by what you are personally as by the place you hold near by what now comprises and will no doubt do so forever, the abyss and the summit, the horror and the beauty of my life— in brief, the sole event of my existence, you are the sole person in the world who will be able to bear witness to what I once was. Is that so all important, you will say to me, that it be known what you were? Not that—no, that isn't what I wanted to say—only that there is always someone to utter, on earth, the human truth of another being, whether this latter be known or unknown to the former, whether this former be known or not by the world. And I know that as far as I am concerned you are the one to whom this ability (should I also say this task?) has been attributed, regardless of whether one day you be required or not to make use of it, in a certain way and for whomever, and for whatever. You will not find it surprising, all the same, that I would instantly cease this display if I did not imagine that the knowledge of what a man has in his heart and in his soul, and of what he was unable to put there, can prove beneficial to the youth of someone like yourself. Pray for your

Mordechai

Mordechai Schamz remembers the fascination exercised upon him when he was young by interesting people. He would have liked not to have lost the fervor of years long past. But has he lost it, all told, or is it people who have lost their personality? Of course, if he asks himself the question, it is to make himself smile a little (now that he likes acting the imbecile). Obviously, he is the one who has grown tired, or not even, who has merely changed his notion of what personality is, or rather of what it ought to be so as to interest him. He changed it, he says? Well, now then he is going to be able to explain in what respect he changed it. Yes, no doubt, for example, nowadays what he likes in people is—honesty. Honesty? Nothing else? Let us accept this. So then those he admired before were not honest? Nothing of the sort; he believed they were honest. What difference shows between those he now thinks are honest? Is it being dishonest to be attractive? And, on the contrary, must a person first be uninteresting to be honest? Ah, deceiver, you are deceived, Mordechai Schamz shouts at once inwardly, and stop pretending to have an interest in the bogus progress of your spurious ideas. You know full well that it is the world that has changed, and there is nobody in it anymore to fascinate you—you know full well that you cannot change without the world, for the reason that the world cannot change without you. Do you think it possible that you can change without others changing, that of these two lives one can stop without the other? You have changed because the world has changed, for the world has changed because you have changed. It is all quite simple to understand. Where would the world be, do you think, without ourselves, where would it be if we were not in it? Then he stopped there. Mordechai Schamz likes at times to fly into spurious, inconsequential fits of anger, but never for very long. Thus calmly it is that he resumes in order to conclude: but you see, where you're fooling yourself yet again is by letting yourself believe that you ever knew what people are.

Passing time, murmurs Mordechai Schamz, his eyes at his feet, as if that was where he saw it passing. Then, lifting his head, gazing vacantly off into space, seeming to follow its trail, he repeats: Passing time. He would really like to form an idea about it, and certainly this is indeed what he is seeking on the ground and in the air. Would it help him if he said it a third time? He says it a third time. But that does not help him. He has trouble, really, coming up with an idea about the thing. Perhaps because he does not see what time passes through. If he were to see objects and people, here, right before him, each and every one transfixed and swept away as if by a gigantic arrow, his doubts would cease to exist, but such, apparently, is not the case. However—is it only with the eyes of the body that one sees?—could he not, he reflects, use those of the imagination to picture all those things surrounding him at the present moment that are irremediably carried off, disappearing from his life forever? Such a thing is easy but changes nothing. Everything is still there. Everything—always? That remains to be seen; might it not be advanced that what he sees there is not what he saw the preceding moment, but on the contrary something absolutely new, arriving to replace what preceded it, and this perpetually and infinitely? Yet nothing has moved. The fact, upon close reflection, far from invalidating the hypothesis that time sweeps away everything with a steady movement, verifies it. For if it only swept away, for example, himself and his gaze while sparing what he embraces, or inversely, it is precisely in that way he would see things changing. But it is the perpetual, simultaneous renewal of his gaze passing away at the same time as its objects which creates the illusion of durability. What about memory then? It also must pass away perpetually and, if so, it can only be a case of pure self-deception, inventing the past in accordance with the present each time it means to confront one with the other. All that is possible, perhaps, but changes nothing about the thing. In point of fact, what is this thing? If I really knew, if for me it was anything other than "passing time" (that is, the very moment), concludes Mordechai Schamz, I would be able to begin to think about it.

For a long time, Mordechai Schamz believed things existed. For him, please understand, for him—never does he forget to be modest. For that matter, perhaps this enormous modesty is what makes things, gradually, vanish from his sight. Not that they are no longer physically present all around him—on the contrary, he surrounds himself with them, revels in them, gorges himself upon them; without them, he does not know what would become of him. The closer they are, the greater his attachment; the same goes for his clothes, daily objects. In this sense, no doubts about their existence; they exist even with a greater and greater tenacity. But this is also the sense in which they vanish. So then they vanish as entities, insofar as he assimilates them, fuses them with himself, transforms them into appendages of sorts? No, they vanish in direct relation to his drawing close to them, to his getting to know them better. Then does knowing them mean knowing their vacuity? Not that either. What is it then? Well, the point is Mordechai Schamz himself does not know. He can only notice their slow and progressive disappearance, even without explaining it to himself. Mention has been made of his modesty. Might it not be possible to search in this direction? Does not what surrounds him and concerns him vanish as his modesty increases and, consequently, as its intrinsic value diminishes? According to this hypothesis, they could just as well grow in the same measure. Grow, yes, why not? toward non-existence, at the same time as he himself—tending, with the same movement as his, toward metaphysical extinction, preceding him by the same margin in advance they had over him at the outset, just as hands are first to vanish at the end of outstretched arms in the fog. This image rather pleases him. Is it sufficient for the hypothesis it illustrates to attain the dignity of an explanation? In point of fact, that scarcely has any importance because the reason of things has never caused them to exist—or not to exist, muses Mordechai Schamz. Whether they disappear like hands in the fog or feet in quicksand—the fact is always there. And then, who knows if they will not reappear?

Come autumn, in the gardens, it is a pleasure to see Mordechai Schamz walking. And as for those who see him, if only they knew it was he, what great satisfaction they would take in watching him. But they do not know who he is—thus they experience no happiness, and he, unperceived, passes before their eyes. He goes along, however, insensible of the fact that he is not stirring interest, large bird, who hardly seems to be walking. Under his steps, the leaves are not disturbed; it is as though he were fluttering. Like birds, very rarely does he stop and seem to survey the surroundings, with his head forever moving and his eyes constantly shifting, rather than strolling along. If someone were there to take an interest in him and have the curiosity to follow him a certain while, this person would first have the impression, upon seeing how with broad lively steps he systematically visits every section of the garden, that he is seeking out something or someone he knows to be found there. This impression would last only as long as he does not return to places already visited. From that moment on, considering how he has altered neither his gait nor his bearing, the observer will conclude that he is merely, and no doubt in his weird way, out for a stroll. Soon, however, the changes he observes in the path he travels, which becomes more and more sinuous, the movements of his head more and more rapid, seem to signal for a second time that he is seeking out something, a thing he has apparently not found the first time around, a search he has for a time abandoned, and which a new idea seemingly inspires him to take up once again. Yet, the observer detects no agitation in his bearing, which might be said to resemble someone's accomplishing a task he is long accustomed to. All told, he gives the very clear impression of verifying that everything is in its place, such as he might have left it during a previous inspection. Perhaps this is the case. The way people bear themselves, even under the most cursory observation, gives rise to any number of interpretations, each not any less or more plausible than any other. So it is, under the eyes of his hypothetical observer, with Mordechai Schamz.

In the streets, where sometimes women cry while the men accompanying them cast guilty, furtive glances their way, Mordechai Schamz watches humanity pass by. Now here is exactly the kind of thought he repents after having no sooner conceived it. Do you even know if you are enough a man to be able to benefit from the same world as those whom you consider to be your fellow creatures? he corrects himself immediately. What have they done, what crime are you aware that they have committed, what do you see on their faces for you to believe they are not only your own fellow creatures, but furthermore, capable of being objects of your ruminations? Mordechai Schamz has always appreciated the bombast of exaggeration and the exaggeration of bombast— he suspects each contains even more truth than he senses is there. In the present case he is unable to really know which, but nevertheless continues in the hope that indignation, upon its wings, will prove able to transport him to such truth. Do you truly believe that your own power of penetration so surpasses their power of being that it is within its capacity to first understand them, and afterwards, like a spider, consume them? Do you think that, just as it does with flies, you can stop them in their course, immobilize and manipulate them at your leisure, in the same way the insect rolls them between its legs, until your thirst for firsthand knowledge is sated? Don't you know they are all endowed with a will to be, with an aspiration toward a better future which cannot abide their coming to a stop in order to add up the things, like an accountant at the end of the month, that deter them and draw them onward, by force or by law—do you believe yourself stronger than their destiny? However, indignation, which cannot be forced for very long, now having abandoned him, it is in the gentler mode of reverie that Mordechai Schamz finds himself obliged to continue: yet if I grant, as pure hypothesis and merely for a moment, that the power of my gaze were to exceed time's itself, thus able to immobilize its objects between past and future in an utopic laboratory where will be found stuck on pins their responsibility, itself stripped of its powers of will and repentance on the one hand, on the other of its attributes of hope and of need, for their part rightly esteemed, would I then still need to be bereft of will and hope which allow time to have a hold over me? No doubt I would be, if I were invisible, cackles Mordechai Schamz inwardly, and with no one able in the street to watch within myself humanity as it passes by.

For a long while now Mordechai Schamz has been wishing to experience a great fear, a real fear; not a definite fear about something concerning him, or about himself, but a fear freed of any personal consideration, and in which his whole being would be engulfed as he contemplated its cause. For a long while he has reflected upon what this cause should be so that it would produce the desired effect. He came to the conclusion that it was absolutely indispensable that it be unimaginable. But is such a thing possible? However unimaginable the most "unimaginable" thing might appear a priori, the imagination will always be able to invent some relationship to ourselves, thus giving rise to a resurgent

41

consciousness of ourselves, which will have been absent as long as the state of surprise lasts. The consciousness of ourselves, whispers Mordechai Schamz, that's it, no doubt whatsoever, that's where the key to the problem lies. What fear can exceed the limits of our imagination as long as its source, the consciousness of ourselves, survives, and in turn protects it? None, that's plain to see. Therefore we must be deprived of the consciousness of ourselves—all the while remaining conscious that we exist. So consequently, here is the adventure that I would need to live through, ideally, in order to experience a fear whose effect would disappear only with the cause: one fine morning, I'm passing by a mirror, whistling, if I knew how to, and—I don't recognize myself. I know it's myself that I'm seeing—that the image which it represents belongs to the being contemplating it, but that's the extent of my knowledge: the mirror shows me that I am not what I had always believed myself to be, that this is what I am without the least knowledge. What is it, I would stammer, what is it—neither stunned nor crushed but simply and wholly reduced to this desperate interrogation, with no chance for any other question to survive. The problem now is to know whether all that is needed to regain my identity is to station myself outside the mirror's range—then, that once determined, to know what would happen if I resumed my position. Fortunately, Mordechai Schamz congratulates himself, there is no end to this kind of questioning. Otherwise, one fine day it might be possible to meet with a certain truth.

Mordechai Schamz is a traitor and he knows it. Traitor to whom, to what, is of no consequence. It is the consciousness of treason that creates treason, the ignominy of the traitor that makes a man a traitor. Even if it so happens that he loses sight of his condition, his sense of honor quickly recalls him to his duty. For, whoever a person is, he must at least do himself the honor of always bearing in mind who he is, and if only one duty exists, it is never to forget this. On the whole, he acquits himself of the task rather well. It must be added that he is greatly helped along in this by nearly everything his eyes or thoughts fall upon. Traitor, traitor, so signify for him each day the thousand little things making a day what it is, and to leave no words unspoken, these thousand little invectives are precisely what make a day what it is for him. He would be in no position to assert that he could do without this. If, however, on very rare occasions he happens to experience a certain listlessness before such unvarying words and tones, he swiftly dispels it, and consequently the desire to remedy its cause, by remarking to himself that first of all he is unable to accomplish anything of the sort, since he does not know the cause, and secondly, that if its nature had been revealed to him and he were thus empowered to change it, he would no doubt be simply exchanging one form of treason for another—if only by his betrayal of the previous condition —and all this without any way of knowing whether it would help or harm the cause. Perhaps, indeed, it is a bad thing, a harmful thing, quite unsympathetic, in a word, a truly black thing, for him to commit treason. Of course this uncertainty and the paralysis to which, all possibilities once considered, it reduces him, weighs on him at times and leads him, in rare moments of distraction, to dream that a man, one day, stops him in the street and takes him by the shoulders to announce: Mordechai Schamz, you are not a traitor. But in no time he pulls himself out of his daydream with the thought that, even though this providential stranger would perhaps be able to understand everything about him a person comes to know through experience, nevertheless the experience of his treason stems from the understanding a person acquires by not experiencing something.

Mordechai Schamz singularly lacks presence of mind. Let a passerby stop him on the street to ask for directions and look how flustered he gets, stuttering, wandering off the point. The city suddenly strikes him as an endless labyrinth where you could find yourself only after expending superhuman efforts—at the very least beyond his reach. Yet, he knows, he knows full well where the fellow wants to go. He would be, in other circumstances, quite capable of indicating to him the path to follow—the best, the shortest—in a few perfectly constructed sentences. But here, point-blank and unprepared, so to speak, he can only plead ignorance and proceed on as fast as possible. Certainly this ridiculous inability does not fail to try his patience. Where was my mind at, he takes himself to task, at the very moment I needed it? Was it all so far away that it could not come back? And in the depths of what wondrous regions that it did not deign to return here above to assist me? What better had I to make it do, at the time, than to inform that poor passerby? Oh! I'm rather sorry for him—and even more so for myself. For who knows if it is not always like this, if my mind always finds itself where it ought not to be without me knowing despite everything where it is, and that I draw no benefit from this roaming about, inopportune as it is useless? Now the matter appears to me clearly with particular thanks to an emergency—but is not life itself a continual emergency, necessitating its presence in a permanent manner? It is quite possible that I find myself unawares in a constant state of inability to react to its solicitations—and the fact I only perceive all so few, that it seems to me marked by a great placidity, one full of mercy toward me, could rather be the proof to the contrary. Thus I would live all the hours in my life as I lived a short while ago, that minute in the street, the difference being that I would not even be conscious of the need to answer the questions put to me? Ah, the matter merits reflection, Mordechai Schamz says to himself with a smile. But how to accord it with such a mind that is never where it ought to be? His smile broadens, and he almost even laughs.

Mordechai Schamz doesn't know how to do all that much with his ten fingers. It gets to the point at times that one wonders how he performs the simplest operations. Objects seem wary of him, unless he is the one who is wary of objects. It is always difficult to determine the share of responsibility in dual relationships. If they are the ones wary of him, why? Might he possibly be brutal? On the contrary, he has always shown them a delicacy so great it verges upon circumspection. Might it then be that he is not bold enough, and that they turn to their benefit what perhaps seems a kind of fear? Afraid, however, is something he is not: respectful, certainly, as toward everything that occupies this earth, but he was never a coward. Yet he must admit that if he were to conduct himself in a cowardly fashion it would rather be toward them than to those who resemble him. Is not a challenge, he muses, more imposing than that movement and shouts contained in the very placid inertia of such matter? No doubt, if I needed to defend myself against something here below, I would be far more helpless faced with something whose motives and weapons are equally unknown to me. To such an extent are they unknown, as a matter of fact, that I would be rather hard put to discover if they hold anything against me. Thus, if at this moment I were to be besieged on all sides and near to succumbing, I would not even perceive it. Such is the immense advantage they have over me: in the war they would wage against me—that they are perhaps waging against me or, rather, that they have waged—I could be dead, I am wounded, I have already been vanquished and enslaved for a long while perhaps without ever having had occasion to learn that I needed to defend myself. Anyway, it doesn't much matter, since I don't feel the effects of it. The imagination is a thing as beautiful as it is dangerous. Thanks to it, here is Mordechai Schamz primed to suffer the chains of the inanimate. Small surprise that afterwards I am so clumsy, he says to himself, if my hands are not free due to wearing them. Unless they bear the orb and scepter, the insignia of my sovereignty over them.

From Mordechai S. to G.

My Adored One,

Do you believe such a thing is possible: that it is your kindness which is my downfall? At times I do think so—without actually believing it, I mean. Here is the substance of what I say to myself: if he abandoned me, then I would have no hope. And from the depth of this despondency, who knows if I would not be at last capable of mattering to you? To insult you, to threaten you, to abominate you, but not to be unaware of you. You know that I am not the sort of man who lets himself be deluded; this is my only reality here below. Thus how well I know that I am unaware of you, just as the man who knows himself to be loved can be unaware of her by whom he is loved—he knows himself to be loved, and that suffices him. But if he was no longer loved, what would happen to him? This is more or less the trial I am hoping for. Please understand me however: I know myself to be loved but you know that I cannot feel the effects of your love. Thus, by my own fault, you do not fill me with your presence for I merely sense it, while it seems to me that your absence, on the contrary, fills me with a horrifying tranquillity which at last makes me experience you through my want, whereas I have only known you through the excess of your compassion. If you were able to love me in a way commensurate with my love, then yes, I would be able to love you. On the other hand, your failure to be present in the place where you are no longer is something I would prove worthy, not to mention that I alone would reside there. All this, of course, is mere speculation, and I cannot know in what way I would behave in your absence. But is there not but one failing and one fault in the world: not to love? Is it not preferable to relieve oneself in suffering than to bear the weight of it in useless suffering? For there is only one remedy for the failure to love: love; suffering without love is only an intensification of this failure. And it is truly because my suffering caused by not loving you is useless that, as is the case with my useless love, I have knowledge of it without, if I may say so, the exercise of it. But hardly have I begun to speak to you than I no longer know what I am saying, than everything is lost in your immensity.

Mordechai

What sort of life can Mordechai Schamz live? What sort of life can he accept? If someone were to take an interest in him, that's no doubt the first question he would ask himself. It takes another to know if he would obtain a response. Indeed, drawn from where? From himself, from this shadow which passes and will never stop? Most likely not. From his own reflection then, but based on what data? Discounting this shadow which passes, he has none. Now the question is therefore settled, if it has so much as been asked, considering that there is no one whom he might interest, perhaps precisely for the very reason that he does not seem to exist sufficiently to possess the capability of attracting a life to him, the way one charms a woman or a snake. Yes, life is a woman, he says to himself in the rare moments when he takes an interest in himself, what life needs is charm, mystery and through these, a fondness for her, and what have I of such things? Or on the contrary, like bashful lovers, I perhaps feel toward her too much respect and attraction to dare attempt seducing her. Yet I had better choose between one or the other of these propositions. I cannot remain between the two. And why not? What is it that I cannot do in the end? In my imagination, I can quite well see myself running from one to the other, going relentlessly from indifference to a love that blazes until it consumes itself. It would be a tumultuous way of remaining motionless between the two, and satisfying as well, if what is important in life is considered to be movement. Perfect: here I am in imagination—that's the essential thing. But have I imagined her? Well no, I've forgotten again. And afterwards would I like her to belong to me, be faithful to me, whereas all I do is think about myself? But what an idea, to think about life without me. Yet that is something I can do, just as thinking about myself. But both at the same time, that is asking too much of me. Nevertheless, what is life without me and I without life? It is nothing—and yet I conceive of it, whereas I cannot conceive of what in this instance is opposed to it, namely reality. Had I better conclude, muses Mordechai Schamz, that I can only think this nothing and that everything that I cannot think is its opposite?

Mordechai Schamz does not wait. Not that he is impatient—
but this is not a question of character, merely of nature.
Nature, admirably, made him in such a way that he does not
wait and, it might even be said, in order that he not wait. For
what reason, it alone knows, but as we always like to adapt to
what is imposed upon us, Mordechai Schamz says to himself: Why should I wait? Whatever is supposed to happen to
me, that will surely be mine when the time comes, whether I
wait or not. And then, by waiting, you go against the nature
of time, which never waits. That is at the very least inhar-
monious and perhaps even noxious. Might as well do as it
does, and move on. You then feel that you have a traveling
companion of sorts, a kind of comrade at whose side you take
part in an action—thus you feel that you form half of a pair,
responsible for half, which is far from being negligible.
Whereas if I were waiting there, arms crossed, more or less
with my back against time, it would have a slight air of
bravado which is ill-suited to my humility. I would look like
I do not approve of what is happening, of keeping in my
possession, for myself alone, some sort of grandiose project,
as if such a thing were possible—as if, inevitably, the project
one day would not need to meet up with time and be thrown
in it. Just as well to do so right off; the matter is far simpler
and far less painful. Thus, no sooner does he find himself in
possession of something through the workings of this unex-
plainable phenomenon that causes what is not us to spring
from within us, than he hastens to throw it into time. He
experiences untold delights seeing the thing, still warm
from his touch, accompany him an instant, only to instantly
disappear before his eyes, drawn along, according to its
weight and what it chances upon along the way, either toward

the bottom or backward or forward. So that, if Mordechai Schamz's attitude toward time needed illustration, he would best be shown as a conjuring explorer, constantly pulling from the bottom of his light pirogue objects of every nature and size which he immediately surrenders to the current that draws him along with a movement as steady as it is invariable.

The eventuality of old age smiles upon Mordechai Schamz. Without giving himself any reasons, its drawbacks appear to him as advantages. There are days when he would like to have already arrived there, and the enfeeblement of his faculties, the loss of his means, strike him, as opposed to degeneration, rather as a sort of culmination. Why then, otherwise, would we live so many years before attaining it? he remarks. It must be seen, due to the sheer difficulty we had in doing it, and in proportion, a reward. What's more, if youth were such a beautiful thing, it ought to be given to us, quite obviously, last of all, after we would have learned to enjoy it. On the contrary, we embark upon it deficient in experience and hardly have we begun to form an idea for ourselves of what living is all about than we have left it. It is strange that my fellow creatures have not noticed some sort of contradiction in that. Do we begin with what is best? Has the advice ever been given to eat your cake first of all? And should it be any different with life, by any means not the least of delights? The misapprehension perhaps derives precisely from the fact that it is not generally considered as such. The unfortunate trouble is that this is precisely how it needs to be thought of before all else, so that afterwards there is a chance its end will be recognized as its apogee—and such, until now, does not seem to be the case. How many things are there, however, generally considered as desirable, good, delightful, but experienced by individuals with as much diversity as life is itself? For what reason should this life not enjoy the same prejudices as success, wealth, fame, etc.? You're forced to believe, as the popular saying goes, that life was not present the day the prizes were awarded; otherwise the same eye would be cast upon those who complain about it as upon those who would deplore the above-mentioned states, and many of whom are no doubt wary due to the simple fear of going against the established truths. But perhaps I am thinking so freely, muses Mordechai Schamz, because it has never been my lot to meet with any such truths.

At times Mordechai Schamz is tempted. Each time it manifests itself in an identical manner: he is seized by a vague anxiety, which he knows he would be able to remedy on the spot if he allowed himself to be induced to acquire a knowledge of his nature, which he will not do in any case, for this is where he recognizes the temptation. The remedy to evil lies in the knowledge of it, but in this knowledge also lies temptation. The temptation is the remedy by means of knowledge —in brief, the knowledge of evil plain and simple. Might this evil be a good, so that he feels the need not to remedy it—and the temptation to do so? How can this be known, since he could only do so by yielding to the temptation? Thus it is in the end that the temptation consists in finding out if the evil is a good—or an evil, that is, whether it is good or not to bear it. But where does he get, all told, the idea that this altogether legitimate desire is a temptation? It seems therein lies the real question: for what reason is the need to remedy his anxiety a temptation? Why is this temptation indeed a temptation?

There, consequently, is the genuine temptation—in the desire to know his nature. If it is so, the conclusion is that it resides only within itself, that it has as goal and cause solely itself, that it is pure temptation, pure and simple temptation. If its source is itself, this source nevertheless needs a field of activity. And this field can be no other than himself. The temptation would therefore be purely from himself: the temptation of himself. From himself arising before himself as a self-temptation. A new definition which brings him back to the point of departure in the guise of a new question: in what respect can he be a temptation to himself? To this question is not knowledge once again the only possible response? What else can he do to place himself purely before himself, if not tempt himself to find within himself a solution to his need to know himself? It is fortunate that to this ultimate form of temptation, remarks Mordechai Schamz, I am not even tempted to yield.

Mordechai Schamz knows there is something happening. Deep down inside he is absolutely certain about it. Only he doesn't manage to make it rise to the surface. What prevents me? he asks himself. Perhaps, above all, the fact that once I've brought it to the surface I will not know what to do with it, that is, exactly where to place it. Indeed, something is happening, that is for sure, but where? On the surface or in the depths—off to the side or within? It would still be necessary to know on the inside of what space. And even whether it is a space that must be sought, or rather a time. Might not it well be supposed that two times exist in a parallel manner: one that I would be able to call, for example, my own and where, in its various guises, event, in succession, occurs, and another where time is conferred with its essence simultaneously with its meaning, where it takes root and reaches culmination? Still it would be necessary, for it to prove of any use to me, that they merge into each other at a certain moment. However their fusion abolishes their difference, even if it came about for a billionth of a second, for no such time exists from which an instant can be subtracted or modified. So much for time. What about space now? It is the same: what applies to time just as well applies to space. Thus here I am deprived of time and space, of the superficial and the profound, unless such be within me. And that's where I will need to come back once again. Let us therefore start over. I am deep inside absolutely certain something is happening but this certainty is not communicated on the level where things are happening. In other words, my observation of an event does not show any solidarity with my belief in this event and vice versa. Indeed, as opposed to Thomas, I believe only what I do not see. I have no choice but to conclude, concludes Mordechai Schamz, in an exceptional incapacity. But on the other hand I can take delight in this exceptionalness: no doubt, if the rest of my fellow creatures were to find themselves in my position, I would not even have the opportunity to worry myself about it.

Joy, Mordechai Schamz says to himself, joy, oh joy! But he does not quite know what he means by that. Still, it does him good. He experiences something like joy. Then it is because that means something for me, he remarks, since I say to myself I feel something approaching it. But on the other hand, how can I say it approaches it since I don't know what it is approaching? I experience a feeling, that's all; and I have no need to say what it approaches. I have no need to do so and yet so have I done—therefore it must correspond to a reality of sorts, for a thing that does not exist cannot be noted if there is not at least the need for it. Then joy must exist since I note, without the need to do so, that the feeling I experience approaches it. It exists, but in my sole capacity to approach it, which is in equal measure my incapacity to seize upon it. In the end, it is as if this joy refused to accept only my definition, as if it were present, but anonymously. However, how can a thing I experience refuse to accept my definition? If it were to exist in itself, I would understand it, but a feeling that belongs to me only exists through the definition I confer upon it; it does not exist outside of myself, nor its definition outside of my intellection. Should I infer from the preceding, continues Mordechai Schamz, that joy does not exist since it cannot be subjected to my defining faculty? So I should, so therefore I must; so I must, so therefore I will; so I will, so therefore I do. It is done. However—joy! All I need do is to utter that word for my arms to rise, for me to whirl around and gambol on the spot, and turn my face up toward the sky and, even if it be the ceiling, see the heavens there. It is strange, all the same, a word, without definition. Perhaps that is the reason words are made. And in that case they are well made, for what more can one ask of them? At least not the definition that we alone can give them and which they seem to do without quite well. What would it be, then, muses Mordechai Schamz, if I had said, instead of joy, *elation*. Elation.

Something has remained in Mordechai Schamz of his childish obsession with symmetry. To know how he understands such a notion means finding out what he has up his sleeve. It is on this very subject of sleeves that he evokes these distant memories. Those sleeves, he has been told, were his chief worry. He spent, according to some stories, hour upon hour comparing the length of one arm to the other. He was, apparently, a very strange child who drew no satisfaction from the disequilibrium of the world. In this respect, what has survived is that, if he tolerates movement, it is only by considering it as a state of transition from one equilibrium to another. A motionless movement, that is what would fully satisfy him. And as he is not the sort of man to tolerate for any length of time being far removed from his satisfaction, he applies his mind to recognizing, as far as he is able, immobility in movement. He is very capable of doing so, and on numerous occasions. Is not the mind made, he reflects, as much to satisfy us as to guide us? What's more, toward what can it guide us if not satisfaction? From which, what's more, results that the quest for satisfaction is life's great journey. If it could not be found, no man would have the idea of searching for it. And what is the search for it if not movement, and what is its discovery if not immobility? Because searching for it means needing to move and having found it means not having to move anymore. From which follows logically that not having to move anymore means to have found it. Thus all it would take is not moving anymore in order to find it, if we alone were responsible for our movement, which, unfortunately, consists in two utterly distinct facts: that of moving from one place to another ourselves and that of being ourselves displaced. We have a power over the first and not over the second. So that at the moment when I set my mind to seek satisfaction by perceiving immobility beyond movement, my mind is itself in motion upon time. However, what obliges me to recognize this movement if not my mind? That would tend to prove, muses Mordechai Schamz, that it is not entirely dedicated to my satisfaction.

Mordechai Schamz would not be averse to being a polisher, especially of shoes. He likes the energetic movement of the brush which wrestles a gloss from dullness. This activity is marked neither by accidents nor mystery, and its brilliant result always seems, in proportion to the expended effort, a somewhat undeserved reward. Thus he would ask for very little in cost for his services and he would find himself extremely busy. That would not bother him either, remaining bowed over his folding stool a greater part of the day, without almost ever having the time to raise his eyes toward his customer's. He is sure that he would in this way develop a rough science of mankind through its shoes, which quick glimpses and rare questions introduced at the right moment would refine to the point of infallibility, insofar as such a quality can characterize the knowledge of a subject so extensive and so mercurial. Evidently, muses Mordechai Schamz, the choice of such a point of view restricts the field of investigation, but not its possibilities of development. And who knows how far, given years and patience, it will lead me? Is there an end to any sort of investigation whatsoever? There is nothing, until now, to prove it so to us, and the goal is only defined once it has been attained. Thus, mankind is merely a vain word as long as it has not been wholly grasped by a body of knowledge and, by whatever end it has been laid hold of—brain or shoe—you never arrive at anything before arriving once and for all. Here is why I can, beginning tomorrow, throw myself, if I so desire, into the knowledge of mankind through its shoes, with as much chance as any other person to be the first to arrive, regardless of the head start he has upon me or the path he has chosen. Mordechai Schamz raises his head; he gazes vacantly, and a half-smile traces itself on his lips while he imagines himself on his folding stool set up on some street corner, bowed the whole day long, and in all sorts of weather, in his pursuit of the unknown which hides in all those whose feet he busies himself about.

Oh! if only Mordechai Schamz's infamy were revealed, he would draw great benefit from it. For if he fears the opprobrium which the inherent justice of life might one day heap upon him, he suffers even more by dreading such a day. However, fear is made of denser stuff than suffering, which is more easily diluted, resulting in that it flows, as do the days, and along with them, whereas fear, similar to a huge chunk of rock obstructing the way, must be confronted all at once. Thus he is confined to calling for the day of revelation in his deepmost wishes, without daring to hurry its arrival. Can I do so, for that matter? he rightly remarks. My destiny is not something I'm the master of; it, rather, is mine. And would I want to force it by shouting my infamy in the streets in such a way that I would not be believed? Is anybody who shouts at passersby taken seriously? Most importantly I would need to believe myself, which I know I do not yet have it in me to do. For if my infamy is obvious to me, such as light itself is, what trouble I would have both explaining and proving it. Am I still too small for it, or is it too large for me? Would it be a good thing for me to raise myself to its level, a bad thing for it to lower itself to my level, or the opposite? I must confess to myself that I am confined to following questions with questions in succession, at least until that day. It may be that we suit each other perfectly, and the fact we are placed in each other's presence is due merely to the workings of time. Perhaps time, which can neither be slowed nor hastened and holds in its possession every denouement, is the one not ready. And in such a case, what am I to do? he notes with relief. On the other hand, Mordechai Schamz would not be unhappy to acquire a bit of a head start in the eventuality, plausible after all, when, come the day, it would be the ignominy of all men that should be revealed. With each and every one, then, taking each other as mutual witnesses, in the surrounding din he would risk not being heard.

From Mordechai S. to Olympe T.

My Dearest,

How are you, and your dear family? Do you know something strange? That is the place, and the way, I best remember her in the midst of your ... of her own family. And do you know a far stranger thing? Despite everything, and all this time, I still consider, more than ever, this family as my own, to the extent, I mean, to which I can consider myself as belonging to anything whatsoever, and anything whatsoever as belonging to me, that is, to a rather limited extent, at the very least. Of course, I cannot belong to anything anymore, and nothing can any longer belong to me but, in this area of life where my sole desire has a right to intervene, I am, in a time that precludes time, with her and you, always in our family. Well, no. Why lie to myself? Why, above all, lie to you? It is not true. Everything has passed. It was, but it has passed. I am no longer part of anything, nor do I belong to anything, and the lingering memories of what I once was part of are lighter than the most distant clouds, and they belong to a sky that no longer exists. Excuse me, but I genuinely believed what I wrote at the time I did so. It is just that perhaps, at times, without me knowing it, my starkness is no longer tolerable to me, that I can no longer conceive of being not only naked but also at every instant stripped of the clothing that I must every following instant once again invent. Invent! Oh my good darling, believe me I pay its just cost through horrible torment. You can have no conception, you who, justifiably, are and have of what it is to have nothing of oneself for oneself, of being nothing to oneself and of needing, without any respite, to seek what all around can be taken, stolen, pilfered, in order to advance in time like a being with a fellow likeness—a likeness only—to other beings. Sisyphus has his rock and he is in luck, since this rock is not himself, but I have time, which is myself. On this mythological note, of such great simplicity, I kiss you, hug you, my indispensable one, as if I were able to do it as once I did in time—past.

Your Mordechai

It so happens that Mordechai Schamz has moments of over-flowing euphoria. What does that actually mean, and is it even possible? he asks himself. Might I be a container that a content could overflow? If I grant that, I must also observe that what leaves my limits no longer belongs to me and that consequently nothing can overflow me. No, if man is limited, it is not in the image of a receptacle, for his capacity to be would in this case be reduced to his capacity to possess, whereas on the contrary he is what he experiences without possessing it and it is precisely his incapacity to contain what he receives which results in him being able to experi-ence so much. Just let me glance at the sky, and now every-thing I can see of the sky is myself; then, just let me turn my eyes away and settle my gaze upon a painting, and this latter entirely fills me, for of the sky nothing has remained. So that if I had to see myself in imagination, it would not be in the guise of a bucket but rather of a hollow cylinder whose ability to hold a volume is nil and whose receptive capacity is unlimited. This image is for that matter all the more appropriate in that it is refined—the exterior surface of a cylinder can, in fact, be assimilated to the opaque, non-conscious surface that man presents to the world, and the inner surface to his conscious, reflective surface, if I may be so bold. Well, of course, I can be so bold, exclaims Mordechai Schamz inwardly, as if somebody were going to rap me on hands, as in the good old days! I can see myself in imagination in all matters I wish; it will do harm to no one, not even to myself. Ah! If it were possible to suffer, he muses, like rats in their labyrinth each time a wrong path is taken, things would be far simpler; and if this is not the way things are, most likely the reason is that we trace our path step by step as we advance, or rather—to keep to my cylindrical conception of being—that it molds us step by step while traversing us. In this sense, the euphoria I happen to experience is in every respect comparable, for example, to the powerful, joyous sound that a shepherd up in the mountain pastures produces when he blows his horn.

At times Mordechai Schamz thinks he already ought to be dead. I must have dawdled on the way and fallen behind, he says to himself. Indeed, if I am not mistaken, all around me I see the signs that I have spent my time. But if I have spent my time, that means I am then ahead. Oh, the matter is more complicated than it appears. For it seems that I am behind my time and ahead of my life. Is such a thing possible? Can life and time be separated? Is it conceivable that the time of a life exceeds a life, that a life exceeds its time? If I take it from myself, it is perhaps not conceivable but quite possible: what is there left me to do? Yes—but also what have I ever done? A bit of harm, no doubt, but that was perhaps what I needed to do—and if there is nothing left me to do, not even a bit of harm, it is perhaps this nothing that is left me to do. What I think of my life, what I reckon it is or ought to be is one thing, no doubt, but not my life. My life is—my life is what I do not know it is. And perhaps that is precisely what life is: your very ignorance of life—every and anything, except what you believe or think or hope that it is. As a matter of fact, is not such in line with the straight and narrow path of things, which wants that far less be known about them than known, and some of the most important things at that? And if I knew what my life is, what more would I do with it than it already does? Have I not lived, and is not that, as far as matters relating to life go, the chief, the essential point—the whole point, even? It therefore appears that the roles are clearly divided: on the one side, it is a question, for life, to occupy its time, what, in all probability, it does not neglect to do and, on the other, for man to occupy his life, it being unimportant other than for himself, whether he do good or harm, hardly any or none at all. If he passes it with the thought that he is not living, that is his business, but not his life—it is his life, in a sense, of course, it is his life, but not his own. So, in short, I understand myself, smiles Mordechai Schamz.

At times Mordechai Schamz feels his consciousness, like a bird, caress him with the breeze of its wing. Not that he is thinking at such a moment about something in particular, or which has some relation to his consciousness—quite the opposite is the case: it might well be said that he is thinking of nothing, if such a thing were possible. The phenomenon apparently bears no relation to his thought nor to his activity which, at any rate, with a few exceptions here and there, is virtually nil. It is exactly as if his consciousness, at such times, were paying him a visit, were simply making him again remember its existence. On his side, he does not make all that much effort to recall himself to it. He does not precisely seek to avoid it; rather it seems that he keeps it in reserve, like a sincere and faithful friend of whom it is enough to know he can be counted on if necessary. Certainly, if this latter were to become pressing, he would not hesitate to call upon his consciousness, but the very least that can be said is that he has only rare need of it. Indeed, he has no more need of his consciousness than animals of men. Animals fly through the air and stop on trees, run along the ground and rest in the bushes and thus, in his own fashion, in the streets and amidst men, does Mordechai Schamz—the place where he lives, feeds, and dwells is in the great desert of himself. No doubt, it is insofar as he is close to his fellow creatures that man needs his consciousness, and in this respect, he can hardly be called a man. Thus he would only have use of it unless he multiplied himself into as many obstacles for himself, which he carefully avoids doing. Is it not more joyous and lighter to awaken every day to contemplate an expanse whose serene regularity is not eventually deformed by any protuberance and where the very horizon has no place, since it is limited by time alone? That is why it is exactly in the way a bird brushes past some other animal that his consciousness, at times, makes itself known to Mordechai Schamz.

Often Mordechai Schamz plays at being another, as when he was a child; he can be a surgeon, sewer worker, a pastry chef, a pope. But the character he prefers above all others, and which he never wearies incarnating, is Prometheus. He can remain an hour at a time, and longer, on his chair in the middle of his room in the supposed pose of his favorite hero. The moment he invariably chooses to live is the twelfth hour after the bird of prey's visit, at which time, the pain beginning to abate, the wait for the coming torture gradually establishes its hold. Oh! the pain, was it not preferable when it alone existed and was omnipotent? he then asks himself. I had no choice to make, being wholly enthralled by it, but now that a part of myself comes back to me, it is only all the better to make me suffer, rendering me my freedom, which is only the freedom to choose between past suffering and that to come. What pain is more bearable—that which is present or that which is absent? But this question will remain without an answer for here I am at the terrible hour when power is given me to choose between them but not to dispose of them: scarcely have I abandoned myself to one pain than the other strikes me as preferable and I am shuttled from one to the other as if by a mechanical movement wherein my freedom no longer has a place, although it itself is the driving force. Thus, this very freedom is the worst of pains, for it deprives me of the only solace I may hope for, that of growing accustomed to it. A long while after he freed himself from his bonds, Mordechai Schamz remains pensive. I dare not see in imagination, he muses, what my life would be if I were not accustomed to my freedom. This little game, however painful it may appear, is nevertheless the most salutary of exercises: it reminds him—no doubt in an excessive way, but one which all the more suits his state of excessive freedom—what life can be, whose habit he has at times a tendency to lose.

Here is a strange adventure that happened to Mordechai Schamz. He was seated on one of his dear benches in one of his dear gardens when a little girl passed by with her mother holding her by the hand. The little girl stopped before him, thus forcing her mother to do likewise, looked at him with surprise, pointed to him with her finger, turned toward her mother, said to her, "That's the man," and looked at him again, her finger still directed toward him. The mother smiled at her child and, without daring to look at the object of her attention, dragged her along to continue their stroll. Mordechai Schamz had never seen the child; he had no doubt therefore that her intercession was merely an occasion to exercise a newfound power of denomination, a phenomenon frequently observed. This child, he said to himself, pointed me out as if she knew me, or accused me, or elected me, and I grant it no importance whatsoever. If it be so, the reason is that she is a child, and in view of her age I permit myself to decide in her place the causes motivating her. But if she were ten or fifteen years older, such a thing would have been impossible for me and I would then have been obliged to seek other explanations entirely for her attitude. Are ten years adequate to allow me to explain with a single thought a fact objectively so mysterious, or would I not do better to ask myself if there does not exist, throughout the world, a certain number of individuals who innately possess a knowledge of my being different from the one I have empirically accumulated—or even one more complete? Upon closer reflection, the phenomenon strikes me as rather banal and can be observed every day without anyone finding it amazing, concludes Mordechai Schamz. To understand more about someone that you have never seen or to understand something different from what he himself understands about himself, to see more, or otherwise, that he has ever seen—is there not a definition that applies to this, among

64

others, which is called love at first sight?

An awareness of nature is very strong in Mordechai Schamz. The simple sight of a tree can move him to a point he himself will find amazing. If he were not a city dweller, he would live in the country. And why does he not do so for that matter? In other words, what holds him in the city? Its gardens, how absurd, he shouts inwardly. If I were told of someone who likes nature and has every opportunity to settle in the country, and that he stays in a city because of its gardens, I would say such a character is mad or that he does not like nature as much as he thinks or claims to, or even that he likes it only in the city. One problem, however—this character is me, and I cannot treat him as lightly as I would any other character, namely by advancing several hypotheses about what is behind his attitude, among which I would not trouble myself to choose. I must decide upon one reason and one alone for this attitude, equivocal at the very least. Yet I ought to readily admit to myself that I feel neither the desire nor the need nor the right. As for why, there can be but two reasons: one is that all hypotheses are verifiable, the other that I am not worth more than any other character, real or fictional. But is that possible? For if in my own eyes I cannot be any more differentiated from everyone else than any person at random, then in whose eyes will I be me, nothing but me, me alone? In sum, myself? Well then, precisely, in the eyes of anyone whomever, to whom I would render like-wise, unless it be to someone else, or even to everyone else, while they themselves would take me for myself, rendering likewise to me. It would be necessary to grant that all men take each other for themselves, with no one person being himself. Wouldn't it be simpler, muses Mordechai Schamz,

to abandon to others my awareness of nature? They will no
doubt take better care of it—and that would radically resolve
the problem.

Darkness has always intrigued Mordechai Schamz. When
night has fallen and the curtains are drawn, and he is there in
his room with the lamp extinguished, he muses, and he
muses very differently than if his lamp were lit. He muses:
What is it about darkness that makes it not just the opposite
of light, what is it about myself that makes me unable to
muse upon darkness in darkness in the same way I would do
in the light? In other terms, what is it about darkness that it
exists not only negatively but positively? In short, what does
it possess peculiar to itself? If I relight the lamp and I picture
this room in darkness, which I am more than able to do,
something will be missing from my representation, and it is
this something that exists in itself in darkness and which
cannot be captured by pure intellection nor found by the
imagination, therefore possessing an objective status, that I
want to discover. Might it not be something which happens
when darkness comes, like rain with clouds, as it were, and
which leaves with it? Something which swoops, like an
eagle, upon arriving and hovers, motionless and hidden,
awaiting the moment to sweep back into the brightness as it
does? But does it simply wait, or does it not act otherwise if
only by its mere presence? In this case, indeed, it would not
be distinguishable from darkness and would not exist. It
must therefore act, or not be. If it acts, apparently it is upon
myself. All I need therefore do is find what it is in light that
distinguishes me from what I am in darkness in order to
discover the answer. What distinguishes me—I have already
established—is my manner of thinking about darkness. This

thing is therefore me and its action my thought. The line of reasoning strikes me as rather well drawn, all things considered, and I can very well see in imagination Mordechai Schamz swooping upon Mordechai Schamz with the darkness, so as to wholly invest him and, once light comes to be, withdrawing from him just as abruptly, so that there is a difference as great and as inconceivable between one and the other as between light and darkness.

There are days when Mordechai Schamz is utterly like a flat tire. Where am I, where then have I passed? he asks himself with as much irony as he can draw up from himself, and in no matter what direction he looks, he can find no answer. But this state in which I find myself, he continues, does it not provide an opportunity for me to pose a question which strikes me as far more fertile, namely, where then was I previously? You cannot see the place you occupy, only the one you *have* occupied. Here then is the ideal moment to contemplate the place I occupied. Still, the place I occupied, if I am no longer there, I cannot see myself there, and the place I occupy is only interesting due to the fact that I am occupying it. Now look how I have let my thought go astray —and in two directions, since, furthermore, for me to see the place I occupy, I must surely be somewhere and where else, if not in the place I occupy and by definition I cannot see? Anyway—thought would not advance if it did not stumble. I am therefore nowhere—I mean in no place I can observe. So it cannot be a question of place but of state. I am in the place I am but scarcely in existence, deflated—*flat* is the right word. If I am flat, I must surely have been inflated previously. But with what air, come from where? I cannot blow it into myself, for then I would never be in want of it. It must therefore be that the source is not in myself. In this case all hypotheses are possible and none verifiable and my only resort, for want of anything better, is to compare this wind that swells me with the one blowing upon the things of matter, as unpredictable as it is powerful, myself being comparable to a windbag whose volume varies in function of the gust's force. Thus our sensation of ourselves, our awareness of being, is this wind, this void, and the more we are filled with it the more our heads swell, whereas as we gradually flatten we shrink from ourselves toward the reality of our state and we feel a void, even though we are full of our own truth. Ought I to find remarkable once again, Mordechai Schamz questions himself, that things appear to be the opposite of what they are?

Mordechai Schamz has the feeling he is a sieve. Certainly, he sees little, but the little he does see passes right through him. He wonders how others manage to retain time and amass its contributions. For him, time seems to act in quite the opposite way: to diminish him as it flows away. Already nothing much is left me, he says to himself; one day I am going to melt away into thin air. One moment I will have been here, the following I will no longer be found. But since no one will be looking for me, it will not make much difference. If not to say any at all. For that matter, I wonder what can still be retaining me. No person, at any rate, if not myself. Am I retaining myself? Perhaps, unawares, as if by my own weight. I must still not be light enough yet. Yet it strikes me I am adequately so. But the fact is that a good many things also seem not to be. Perhaps my thoughts are what still retain me. Yet they do not feel all that heavy to me, seeing the facility with which I move them. They do not even appear to me as thoughts but rather as breezes, light gusts of air that time sends me and which I am as free to grasp as to let go on by. There is perhaps where the problem lies—I ought perhaps to let them all go on by, not even retain, for example, this one: no matter how poor in reason and in reality it is, it is still a thought, a form I deck myself out in; and it is something I oppose to time which otherwise would be able, mingling me in its pure movement, to bear me away. Yes, no doubt, it is not enough not to have a history, Mordechai Schamz says to himself—for the most minuscule thought is a form offered to time that, regardless of whether you like it or not, flows into the mold of a history. And if I do not possess a memorizable sequence of particular events to present to it, the fact nonetheless remains that this continuous piling up of small cages that enclose time ought all the same to figure a human silhouette with such a similarity to others they could not be told apart.

From Mordechai S. to G.

My Adored One,

Does speaking to you about myself also mean speaking about yourself—does speaking to yourself about yourself also mean speaking about me? Speaking to yourself about yourself, no doubt, about yourself within me, through me and, in spite of what I am, like me, is to speak about myself, and only myself, for what knowledge, if not about myself, would I have of you? Thus it is obvious that speaking to you about myself does not mean speaking to you about yourself but it is not certain, as a result, that it then means speaking to you about myself. No doubt I say things to you about myself and I speak to you of someone who speaks to you, and like someone who speaks to you, but is that what I must say to you, and must I say it in such a way? Obviously, you can learn nothing about me that you do not already know; thus my speech concerns no one other than myself. But does not this speech lead me astray—or worse: does not it deceive me? It strikes me today that it can only be a danger. And perhaps I have always realized this and, by speaking to you, I have constantly sought to discover the nature of this danger. And yet no benefit exists which can be drawn from this knowledge. Perhaps this knowledge might even bring me nothing but harm. It is no doubt for that reason that you are anxious to keep me from speech. If ever I heard anything about you, if ever I had been able to hear, it would have consisted of nothing but this: don't speak. Don't speak to me! And even that would have been too much. It would have meant breaking a silence that you never once broke. In silence, Father, you conceived me and in silence also you keep me within you; for me you cannot be outside of silence, and outside of silence I cannot be from you. It is impossible for me to conceive of your will, nor of your ways; now that is most likely why I speak of them—and my speech says this: if it were possible to take a step outside of your will, and of your ways, then speech would be this first, this unique step. And from the moment I would not be able to abolish the act, all that remains is the hope to accomplish the miracle of obliterating its tracks under all those I would have accumulated.

Mordechai

When Mordechai Schamz imagines men in relation to himself, he is only able to picture an enormous crowd. He is greatly vexed by this, at first because he cannot understand the reason, then afterwards because he is unaware of the crowd's attitude toward him, and finally because he doesn't know what place he occupies with regard to the crowd. Is he against, in front of, alongside? He is sure about one thing only: he avoids the mass of staring eyes concentrated upon him. He looks down or to the side. Is this an image, he asks himself, that I am fabricating for myself in order to fault my attitude toward my fellowmen? But what need do I have of an image, and such a crude one at that, in order to picture what I have known for a very long time and which I have no need to picture? No, it strikes me that the correct way of approaching this problem is to regard the image imposing itself on me as more subtle than a symbol and thus more real. I must imagine that this image exists in itself in a way I am unaware of and that it is therefore, in a way I am unaware of, a reality. Which does not necessarily mean that it is the reality of what it represents. Indeed, an image which exists in itself, by this very fact, is not required to be pictured in order to exist; also by this fact, I ought not to concern myself with what it is picturing. I must admit I do come up with some crazy ideas sometimes, Mordechai Schamz tells himself. Now here's an image imposing itself on me and all I can come up with is that I ought not to look upon it as an image but as a reality. How can an image be said to have a reality if it is not looked upon as an image? Why, within myself, quite simply, he retorts, within myself, omnipotent arbiter of my reality. By what right would a man, who ceaselessly transcribes the incidents of his life into images of his destiny, not be able to turn an image of his destiny into an incident in his life? Especially when one knows, concludes Mordechai Schamz, with what eyes man must regard the incidents of his life?

The water—how to put it? Mordechai Schamz asks himself —the spring was flowing, yes, or gushing. The spring was there. It was a point from where the force of life was gushing. If such a thing can be said. It was a point in a place without a precise location, itself unlocalized and called "spring" for convenience and out of tradition. It was a point where life replenished itself in force, in consistency, in splendor, to say it all, to say things fully and to what point this surge "thickened" reality. Such a thickening of reality can be legitimately confused, in certain respects and under certain conditions, with the production of this very reality. Up to a certain point, therefore, it can be said that this spring furnished reality. In the same manner and for this purpose, it perpetually rejuvenated life. Thus life depended entirely on it for its age, for life has no age if not this youth that the spring alone ceaselessly procures for it. Not surprising, it is therefore that life lost its youth and consequently its age from the moment the spring dried up. From that instant life rejoins this world to which it essentially belongs, where time does not exist. From then, there was no longer a question of waiting, of tastes, of haste. All that remained possible was the contemplation of missing boundaries, of an infinity without qualities, finding its point of juncture with ter-restrial dimensions and conceptions within the limits of a human life. Logical it is, also, that beginning from this moment, this very moment no longer exists or, more pre-cisely, has never existed, and that there is no place for the memory of it, nor of what went before it, except by way and through the conventions of the most unbridled imagination; freedom, apparently, and imagination being the sole possible state and function in this world where for that matter they form but a single entity, or activity, unable, in the present case, to be differentiated. Yet, if I were to be made to feel the difference, muses Mordechai Schamz, if it were to be proposed to me that I know once again this difference—from which the spring no doubt gushed and where this desert of fire, this desert of ice, would vanish—I would not want to feel, I would never accept.

Mordechai Schamz is as serious as a pope. He was still at an age when he did not yet know how to talk when he already had this look of imperturbable seriousness, and people said of him, "Mordechai is as serious as a pope." The look he had on his face did not accentuate the disproportion that adult expressions usually cause when worn upon children's physiognomies. It was a look of seriousness, but without any embellishment or condescension, of serene, benign gravity, peculiarly his own, and which recalled, but in a more majestic way, the look given in days past, in their portraits, to boy-kings. He never forced it, no more than he sought to attenuate it and if, through the years, the genuinely surprising character it possessed did diminish, it does not fail to still have an effect upon all those who have occasion to look at him. Inevitably, the curious passerby and the chance interlocutor ask themselves: Through what hidden authority, through what secret power does this man draw a look of that kind? when his eyes, chancing upon his reflection, surprise his face in its natural state and, if it can be said, in action, he too finds himself forced to face questions. Why this serious look? he asks himself. And why, above all, does it always strike me as strange as it is obvious? The most curious thing is still that it is the obviousness that surprises me and the strangeness that appears natural to me. But is not that, after all, less strange than it appears? Is not strangeness, indeed, always more explainable than obviousness? That a sheep has four legs is an obvious fact, but no one has ever given the reason for it, whereas a sheep with five legs is a strange phenomenon that science explains very easily. My strangeness itself is merely a rarity, and a thought process as simple as comparison suffices to account for it, whereas what is as common to me as to everyone else, such as a life, a face, and four limbs, I find nothing to set these against. Thus, my serious look is a rarity when I compare myself to my fellow creatures, but it is in no respect a strange phenomenon, even as it becomes unfathomably strange from the moment I turn it into an obvious fact—that is, when I compare myself to myself; when, namely, concludes Mordechai Schamz, I have nothing to compare myself to.

Mordechai Schamz would like to have to ask for everything and live, as the English say, from hand to mouth. He would spend the whole day long begging for food and a place of shelter for the night. The sun barely risen, his search would start over. For he would exhibit such ingratitude toward his benefactors that he would never find a hand to feed him twice nor a roof to shelter him two nights in a row. Ingratitude is a rather frivolous word to qualify his attitude which would in reality be characterized by such roughness that he would need to count on fear to achieve his ends rather than on mercy. A bad dog is what I'll be, he says to himself, a pariah dog. I'll look mean and mangy, but I wouldn't threaten. I would merely linger on the spot without troubling to give myself any false airs, and the people before me would find themselves naked face to face with man, since my own attitude would not suggest a corresponding one to them. What fun it would be, all the same, to act each day and several times over like a man before men. Now that's something that could not fail to be full of elements at once unexpected and instructive, thus fully satisfying my taste for—my taste for what exactly? Mordechai Schamz suddenly asks himself. As for what has to do with man, I have all I want in myself, and as for human relations, it strikes me that I have far more than enough with myself. Yes, but precisely the problem is that I depend only on myself, and it is exactly as if each morning I were to ask myself not simply for shelter and something to get by on, but for life itself. And that's really what bothers me the most about myself. Whereas if I had to expect everything from others, what relation would I need to preserve with myself? I would no longer have a reason to possess one with the man who gives and preserves, the one who performs the craven task; such a man would no longer be myself. I would not need to hold others in contempt anymore, those humble executioners, who would no longer be up to joining forces for the single purpose of suppressing this sorry reflection I would impose upon them. I would laugh best then, forcing them to adopt the same expression I myself need to each day before the expression I offer to my inner mirror. But wouldn't that be, Mordechai Schamz questions himself, more craven by far to cast off my own upon those poor people who have as much to deal with as I?

It happens to Mordechai Schamz to feel that he is being followed by himself. He feels, as if behind him, very close, there were a potential him, poised to seize and push him aside so as to take his place. No doubt, he remarks, we all know that we are manifold and that certain aspects of ourselves, for want of an opportunity, will never perhaps manifest themselves, but this is not to the point in the present case. What I feel as if awaiting me, in a certain fashion, is not an aspect of myself, but myself in its entirety, who would be capable of replacing me at a moment's notice; in addition, I do not merely suspect his existence or reckon his nature. I know him even while being farther removed from his consciousness than from that of any other of those "aspects of myself" not yet given existence. Meaning that I would recognize him at once if he manifested himself. For he is myself, but a self taking action. Myself, who would take action; myself, if I were to take action, which explains that I am as close to him as I am removed from him and as essentially similar as fundamentally different—and this resulting from the mere fact that I do not act as he would act. Action alone separates us. More precisely, I alone separate myself from action. No, it is not *more precisely* that should be said, Mordechai Schamz corrects himself, but *on the contrary.* I separate myself from myself who would take action not because I do not take action but because I am he who does not take action. We are not different by the fact of not taking action, for that is an easy matter to remedy, but by the fact that I do not take action. Now there is why he who would take action would have to push me completely out of his way, for he cannot take action through me. And whatever action I might invent to attempt a reconciliation could only be illusory, for it would be the doing of he who does not take action. However I really ought to confess that the matter is tempting, and also remember that I have sometimes allowed myself to be tempted. What man is without weakness, Mordechai Schamz consoles himself, before what he sees that he knows? He is like someone dying of hunger before a pastry-shop window. Thus it would be excessively severe on my part to hold it against myself for having, regardless how feebly, tried. Inasmuch as it would be madness to want to start over again.

Mordechai Schamz goes into the barber's. "Hello, monsieur," he says to him, to which the other answers likewise. Then he sits down and the barber begins to cut his hair. He always welcomes him with pleasure for he really likes to cut his hair. He also thinks that the man has a strange face and if he grew a beard on it, he would want to cut that. He has this weird impression that it is made to be cut, that it would be utterly to his advantage if it were presented all by itself, separated from the body. But this is not a morbid impression. It is an aesthetic impression. He cannot help himself; he thinks the man's head is "made for a martyr." Or a murderer perhaps? No, not a murderer. Or then a murderer so completely repentant that his punishment would make a martyr of him. If such are his musings, the reason is that in his view a head of this sort must be capable of harboring the blackest ideas, the gloomiest designs. So gloomy, no doubt, are these designs that they could never be executed, and whose passage into reality would merely render them insipid, warp them. Now there's something that must be very tough, the barber muses, having to preserve in such a limited volume such grand and terrible secrets. In his place I would suffer martyrdom. Perhaps that is what he is indeed doing, and that is why he gives me this impression. Poor customer! his life must really be hard. It doesn't surprise me that he equally has this look of gentleness you see on creatures who have suffered greatly. Who knows if he would not like to cut short his sufferings? That is perhaps why he comes to see me. Clever as he looks, it may be that in me he felt this strange impulse and he hopes, each time, that I will execute what it commands. I am a conscientious man, one who does not hesitate, when the occasion presents itself, to do a little favor, but I fear that this one here falls outside my duties. Yet, it is not at all difficult when you think about it—a slash of the razor and the job is done. But I must not think about it anymore.

Then there is also the fact that I could be completely mistaken. Mordechai Schamz thinks his barber has some really weird ideas.

There are things which are beneath the dignity of Mordechai Schamz. Yes, he declares forcefully, there are things which are beneath my dignity. But I do not know what they are. Thus I cannot keep myself from doing them, and consequently it is possible I do certain things that are undignified. A comical situation if ever there were one, for this ignorance in which I find things beneath my dignity causes me not to know anymore where to situate my dignity and since this latter is indeed characterized only by the level at which it is placed, in the order of things and actions, it follows that I do not even know if I possess any dignity. However, if I do not know, I sense. And if my sense is that some things are beneath my dignity, it is surely because it is somewhere. But now here is something I had not thought of: it is no doubt somewhere, but not necessarily within me—in other terms, it is possible that I have no dignity, that there merely is a dignity about me. A dignity that is not permanently located in my person, but which visits me, after the fashion of a feeling, or of a thought, whenever it so pleases. But what then is dignity, if it is a feeling like any other, if, in its absence, I accomplish a dignified act which would be undignified once dignity enters into the picture. Yet this really is the way I feel it. For if, on the contrary, it were a stable entity within me, a function, it might be said, or a sense like smell, then such as I know myself, I am not certain that, come morning, I would lower myself to rise. Thus it is obvious that I only invoke my feeling of dignity so that it ratifies a decision in the elaboration of which it was not invited to participate, since I must, even before appealing to it, see whether the thing is possible or impossible; and if I were to make such an appeal beforehand, I would not experience it as such, but merely as a possibility or impossibility to accomplish the action envisaged. That is not only obvious but also fortunate, remarks Mordechai Schamz. I would even go so far as to think that it is obvious because fortunate. Is not the feeling of dignity, indeed, an element indispensable to one's well-being, in general, and to my own in particular?

It might be said that life passes over Mordechai Schamz like a rag upon silverware. In any case he has no qualms about thinking it. Thinking it—perhaps not really. It is rather an impression he has, a sensation. If he were to reason on this subject, undoubtedly he would wind up with a different conclusion. Indeed, he says to himself, upon considering what life changes in man, I observe that life changes as much in me. Appearance, thoughts, feelings, etc., nothing escapes, as with all my fellow creatures, and I would need to look at these essential realities as pure illusions in order to maintain that life does not change me. Might I so regard them sincerely? To be frank, I don't believe so. Yet this feeling lingers that life does not fundamentally change me. Is *fundamentally* really the right word? I am not convinced that this problem is a question of levels. If a house is razed, what good does it do the house to preserve its foundations? Rather I believe I would . need to envisage different places or, more precisely, spaces, amends Mordechai Schamz. For if I exist in spaces that are different, communicating only in special ways, then I can perfectly conceive that there is one of them from where I observe the erosion, deformation, grinding, the very blending that time operates in others, upon my own being, without any more distress than if I were contemplating an apple that is in the process of being consumed. In such a place, I would be at utter liberty to consider myself as a candelabra or, more attractively, a statuette cast in the kind of metal requiring, so as to preserve its initial state, the mere ministrations of a rag impregnated with a suitable chemical solution. I would even be able to go farther and advance that my various successive states are what, after grinding and blending, enter into the composition of the matter that preserves the luster of my primitive state, concerning which all that now remains for me to do is determine its size, construction, style and form, concludes Mordechai Schamz with satisfaction.

There is almost nothing Mordechai Schamz likes more than listening to people talk among themselves. Hours on end he can stay on benches, in cafés, at bus stops, his ears entranced. "He who inquires much about the cause is far removed from the cause," said a Sufi sage; and if wisdom had ever guided Mordechai Schamz, he would find in this thought the justification of the fact that he never makes use of any other means but this to find out about the movements that make history operate. But it is the sound, much more than the sense of what is said, which interests him. This noise of the world charms him, lulls him more than the most entrancing melody. He is genuinely enchanted by it, borne away like a cloud by the air, for this current of voices is the cradle where his silence finds at once impetus and rest. What would I be, indeed, he remarks, if my like beings were as I am? I would be a talker as they are now but they would not be, and undoubtedly I would be unable to find in incessant speech the tranquillity procured for me by a permanent muteness. Oh! I can see myself now, he says with a wholly inward laugh, constantly perched on some chance height to harangue the mute crowds who would certainly be even more hard put to garner a meaning from what came out of my mouth than I am today to find some in what reaches me from theirs. I am quite happy and could not congratulate myself more if the situation were completely the reverse. Completely the reverse, really? he suddenly questions himself. The matter requires review. For after all, this state I congratulate myself about being in, does it not entirely reside in the difference alone? And I applaud myself for not being someone who must at all costs give to his fellow creatures a lesson in noise when I am he who wants at all costs to instruct them with a lesson in silence. Once again I verify, notes Mordechai Schamz, that it is in the guise of the greatest humility that the greatest vanity best hides. I will need to find myself a means to keep all the more quiet.

From Mordechai S. to Olympe T.

My Dearest,

For a long, long time have I been reflecting before writing you: what to say to her that I have not said, how to go about amusing her all the same yet without hiding anything about my misery from her, etc.? I realize today (but isn't it so each time?) how pointless this questioning and these scruples are. For all of that, do not believe I am not the least concerned about boring you and am taking you as a mere pretext for a hygienic outburst of sorts. Such is absolutely not the case. I am writing you because you are who you are; I do not write this way to anyone else, and in fact do not write to anyone else at all. It is precisely because it is to you I am writing that I would like to do it otherwise—such as you deserve it, completely. I would like to tell you everything I can say. But that is, as you will acknowledge, impossible. The only fashion in which I would be able to draw closest to this impossibility would be to write nothing to you. You will agree with me, indeed, that a blank page, by the fact it bears no meaning, eliminates so much less from the totality of possible meanings than does a written page. But it would only be a pure intellectual game and you and I do not number among those who play such things. Do you see, you are so real, you still contain in yourself (I say *still* without knowing if it is not forever) so much of life's reality, the greater part of which has already fled me that I am genuinely ashamed to give you news of this world where I am and where the last realities are perhaps but ink, characters and paper. What you might think of this, how you will take it, I will never be able to have the slightest idea. But no doubt you must, from the simple fact that you read it, confer upon it a kind of reality. Who knows if that is not the reason, above all, that I write you, so as to be able to imagine that somewhere my irreality, under your gaze, is transformed, as if by magic, in a certain fashion, into reality?

Your Mordechai

From time to time Mordechai Schamz muses that it would be sweet to have something in life to lean on. A shoulder to rest on, in a fashion. Yes, but from what? All told, he says to himself, it would prove far more useful for me to find something to rest *from* rather than something to rest *upon*. But is it not the same thing, after all, in this life I have emptied of all obstacles? No, not exactly; it would be more accurate to say both are indissociable parts of a whole, both being indispensable to the existence of this whole, which can be metaphorically illustrated by a space trapped between two parallel walls, one of which you would rest against after attacking the other. Now here is something extremely interesting and new, and which moreover greatly helps me, I who have spent so many years emptying out this space, exclaims Mordechai Schamz. Have I really emptied it, in truth, or ought I rather not say that I merely filled it with emptiness? And more: can a space be filled with emptiness? If this space is space, then it is because it has limits—otherwise it would be emptiness, which it is not, for how to explain that emptiness tolerates an exception, which is myself, all the while remaining itself, that is, emptiness? If I had emptied my space, or if I had filled it with emptiness, which is already contradictory, I would be part of this emptiness and I would not be what I am, but rather emptiness. Therefore I must also really then have a space for myself that I would very clearly see contained between the two above-mentioned walls: one being the idea of emptiness, so sought after by myself, and the other my personal emptiness, by myself so populated. So that I throw myself upon one to rest from the other and inversely. Indeed, the one, the sought-after emptiness, being too empty by far for me to be able to find some sort of bump to hang my thought upon, and the other, my emptiness found, being too aswarm by far for me to be able to choose some chance feature emerging from the mass to fix my thought upon, and since I can make an indiscriminating use of one or the other to rest from my indiscriminating attacks against one and the other, I am neither more held nor repulsed by one or the other. What am I complaining about then, concludes Mordechai Schamz, since I have two shoulders to rest upon, and which in addition serve as a battering ram against the limits of this space which they both lean and slam against at the same time?

Mordechai Schamz might feel rather tempted to allow himself to fall into squalor. With pleasure indeed does he imagine the appearance he would rapidly assume, as well as his room, once abandoning himself to this propensity. The trouble is that his personal propensity would rather be toward cleanliness. I am really a queer devil, he says to himself, desiring to yield to a tendency not natural to me. All told, I would like to force myself all the while seeming to abandon myself—to feel in the healthy constraints of effort the perverse delights of abandon and all that for an unknown goal, one which, in addition, at first glance, revolts me. Then why therefore envisage it? Well, is it not this innate taste I have, precisely, for the unknown and the difficult, to which I might even be able to give the name courage? Yet a courage which, however, through some sort of unconscious modesty, could be said to hide under desire; or rather the desire to desire, for this latter does not exist in me in the natural state. But what is the desire to have a desire that you know you do not have, if not a purely abstract feeling, issuing from abstraction only to immediately return to it? Indeed, to have a desire for something is a thing you are pushed toward, to decide something is a thing you push yourself toward, but to have a desire to be pushed toward something is quite simply nothing at all. And now I must kiss my courage good-bye, admits Mordechai Schamz. For that matter, this gives me great consolation since the goal it was supposed to help me pursue is totally negative. Who has ever drawn anything from squalor? No one. But that is no reason for me not to be able to draw anything from it. And if I have proclaimed this experience of squalor useless, it is only because I do not have the courage to attempt it. I have merely veiled my shame in this instance with insincerity. What a fine mess I am in now, and without any great hope of drawing myself from this pitiful state I placed myself in. There might well be a way, which would consist in noting that the desire for a desire, being neither a genuine feeling nor apparently a coherent thought, is derived rather from the realm of dreams, and that this courage, which I have manifested only in dreams, I cannot deny to myself in reality. But I do not know, Mordechai Schamz says to himself, if I would dare use it.

Mordechai Schamz has little taste for originality. If he had to hold forth to himself on this topic, here is what he would say: Has anyone ever been heard to declare, concerning what charms us in the deepest and most lasting way: "It's original"? Who has ever, even in his most demented dreams, thought to so classify birds, flowers, rivers, mountains, and man himself? It strikes me, on the contrary, that their beauty is perceptible to us above all only through their belonging to a category and I ask nothing more in proof than the natural repugnance we experience toward an individual who differs in some feature from those of his species. In short, I will quite readily affirm that if we do have a preference, it is for copies, and I would be perfectly satisfied with myself if I were able to discover that I am the pure and simple replica of an original. For that would be the undeniable proof that a power superior to myself is satisfied with its creation to the point of exactly replicating it and I would then find it simply impossible to refuse being satisfied with myself. Undeniably, the fact of being a duplicate is in itself a self-justification, without requiring any action on my part; none of my thoughts would escape being not only justified but, by its very existence, perfected. No doubt, if my Authentic Copy Certificate had been brought to me, I would be able to go to bed promptly and not budge from it before being carried out, as the saying goes, feet first. Truly, what prevents me from doing so? For nothing tells me that this Certificate was not delivered to me the instant I was born and I would quite legitimately be able to consider as a sufficient proof the impossibility of any refutation. Certainly, from that instant on, neither anyone nor anything would be able to disillusion me, if from that moment it were not my own wish, or if my vanity were not to do so. As a matter of fact, is not vanity so expensive that it costs one a long life of perfect peace? Is this not reason enough that I not be myself?

It happens—although rather rarely—that Mordechai Schamz thinks of great men. So doing, he evokes their stature, their history and the benefits their thoughts and their deeds brought to humanity. Undoubtedly, he muses, it is necessary and even indispensable that certain among us raise ourselves above the common level so as to show others what they are when at their best. Nevertheless, it must be stated that there is a contradiction in the fact that it is to the man who has shown himself different from others that the task falls of being shown to them in example. On the other hand, in order to represent themselves in the eyes of his fellow creatures, I acknowledge that it is easier to designate, instead of a man who is distinguished from them in nothing, someone who has voluntarily designated himself. Yet, would it not be correct that this fact alone eliminates him from the category of possible examples, since by his state he is already different from those with whom he supposedly shares a fellow likeness? However, despite the difficulty in achieving this, I continue to think, maintains Mordechai Schamz, that it would be preferable and especially logical that the example chosen be of a man comparable in every way to his fellow creatures. Certainly, I cannot dismiss the inescapable objection—namely, that he would not be so from the moment that he is chosen. Would it not be possible, then, to institute, as for soldiers, an unknown great man? Each person would thus be able to imagine a great man according to his own idea, one whose image would not be tarnished by the shortcomings inevitable and inherent in what is human and, thus emboldened by this example at once intimate and perfect, he would make efforts to conform himself to it which would in no way be spoiled by the envy felt toward those who have elevated themselves above us or by the vanity driving us to do likewise. But then, reasons Mordechai Schamz, each man would be drawn toward becoming the great man like everyone else whom until now I am the only one to attempt to be, and I would find myself forced to try to become a great man like every other great man.

Summertime, when the windows of his room are wide open and passersby seek out the shade along the sides of buildings, Mordechai Schamz thinks about the heat. Isn't it rather stupid, he remarks, to increase its effect by inviting it inside whereas it is already so present outside? *Invite it*, I said. But did I really invite it, did I decide, at a given moment; for instance, "Now I am going to think about the heat"—isn't it quite the opposite, that the heat, not satisfied with holding sway outside, has imposed itself on my thought? I am, so it strikes me, quite conceited in my belief that I am the one who chooses my thoughts, for if I take this occasion to reflect on the matter a little, it rather appears they are the ones who choose me. The present case is glaring: not satisfied with occupying me outside, the heat invades me within as well, and establishes itself in the form of a thought. As a matter of fact, Mordechai Schamz corrects himself, should I say that it establishes itself with the form of a thought or that it establishes itself plain and simple? For, all told, my thought, rather than creating the heat's presence, merely attests to it. It is a simple indicator of sorts, a signal that the heat has not penetrated inside. And would it not be accurate to say that it is likewise for each thought, for every thought, in this category at any rate? To be quite honest, have I ever verified that my thoughts heeded my invitation, or were a result of my will, or the consequence of a decision on my part? All that needs be considered is the thought itself, its nature and its form, in order to have an idea of what answer to give. This I do believe: heat is a phenomenon created by a certain cause, which manifests itself in such and such a way, etc.; in short, do I submit it to personal modes of investigation or of representation which make it useful or pleasant for me—do I harness it, in a manner, for my own ends? Or isn't perhaps this the way, if thought could be rendered in words, that I ought to represent it: *Ah! such heat—oh hot—heat woah heat!* Which strikes me as being irrefutable proof that the heat is within me, by way of thought, and not for my benefit but only for its own. With the result that I would be more than willing, based upon the evidence as it appears to me, to define thought as the form which all material phenomenon takes in order to penetrate us in a manner other than physical. It would be interesting to see if, by following the process backwards, you could not, first of all, hunt down the phenomenon from within and pursue it on its own turf, the turf of reality. When it's not so warm outside, decides Mordechai Schamz, I'll give it a try.

Wintertime, from behind his windowpanes, when Mordechai Schamz watches the gray sky, the desire to be in summer sometimes comes upon him. Is it possible to be more useless to oneself than I am? he asks himself. Because it is not open to question that I am in winter; and even less so, that no matter what I do, I cannot be in summer. Can I even think for an instant that my desire would be able to so make things that I am not in winter? No, obviously, and yet I am losing precious time by desiring it, time which, furthermore, I would be able to put to use by cheering myself up or at least by considering myself content to be in winter. Without doubt, it would be not simply amusing but, more importantly, informative, to calculate the time I spend every day resisting reality. The time I spend outside of it that I lose denying it, do I not, by this fact, subtract it from the time of reality? And do I not thus add it, accordingly, to the time I must spend here below? Indeed, can I not consider that life is nothing but the time we have to spend in reality and that what we subtract from it is allotted to us all the same? It strikes me that I can, to an extent I deem adequate, decide that there never will be anyone or anything to bring me the proof that I am mistaken. If therefore I maintain my hypothesis, I can rightly compare my life to a journey assigned me. Quite obviously, I am absolutely free to travel it however I wish. But why then not do it in the best possible way, that is, the quickest? These moments I spend outside of reality, I might just as well spend them within, racing along, like a skier on a slope who slows down whereas he could let himself glide along. Would it not be exhilarating, muses Mordechai Schamz, to accept each instant of life such as it is and, in such a state of mind, is not a person supposed to experience the unparalleled sensation of a slalom racer who, oblivious to everything, including himself, keeps in mind only what motions to go through in order to cross the finish line as fast as possible? Life as a race, now that's elating, exclaims Mordechai Schamz, and to greet each instant that comes our way with a curt "yes" so that it'll step aside and let us by, like the "hup!" or the "oof!" of the runner passing the post.

Out of taste, out of habit, out of necessity, Mordechai Schamz is thrifty. In this matter, what's more, he merely obeys the principle governing all that comes naturally. Has anyone ever seen, he remarks, a tree, a bird, or a mammal that was spendthrift? When I put aside what remains of my meal for a next time, I act exactly as does the lion who does not relinquish his prey until he has entirely devoured it, and insofar as I am satisfied by everything which is the least expensive I am equally comparable to him for whom the best prey is the easiest. No doubt he would laugh, such a person to whom I would maintain that I act in a grocery store just as the king of beasts does among a herd of zebus. It is however indisputable that I am right on all points and that the secret, marvelous, incredible correspondences that link together the beings and things of this earth are so numerous that there will be a long way to go before a total inventory of such correspondences is ever made; and the majority of men lose much in happiness and in satisfaction by not seeking what attaches them, in an often flagrant fashion, to what they deem so far removed from their nature. Thus, to confine myself to my example, pursues Mordechai Schamz, this poor bugger who, just like me, sees himself forced to sad and fastidious calculations before the most trifling merchandise, would be, just like me, the proudest of human beings if he knew that, by so doing, his action is modeled on that of the lion or royal eagle. And is it not, on the contrary, at the very least a discomfort that should rightly be experienced by him who, at the same moment, procures in good conscience and at a price he is heedless of, more than he will be able to consume—disobeying, by this act, the laws which, from the course of the stars to the appetite of the starling, govern the universe wholly and entirely? Upon close reflection, it is fortunate for him that he knows nothing of his disobedience, in the same way that it is unfortunate for the thrifty man to be unaware that he acts in harmony with what commands the alternation of day and night, so that through ignorance one loses and the other wins although they stand before knowledge on an equal footing and, when all is said and done, nothing, by that, is changed. It is really too bad that I can do nothing about it, concludes Mordechai Schamz, but no doubt my capacity to be satisfied with what I have and am has been given me in exchange for the power to change nothing about it, as with all other things.

It is not unusual for people in the street to smile at Mordechai Schamz. Are they smiling at me, he asks himself, or at the sight of me? It's worth raising the question because there is quite a difference between the two. If they are smiling at me it is because, in a certain way, they know me, and because they at least recognize in me something that pleases them or makes them happy; if they are smiling at the sight of me, it is simply because I amuse them. But how can they know me when I have never seen them before? They cannot, quite obviously. Therefore, the reason is that I amuse them. But exactly how, honestly, I could not say. From time to time I catch sight of myself and even take a look at myself, and never once has this brought the slightest smile to my lips. So couldn't it be said that I am the one who doesn't know myself, based on the fact that I am unable to see in myself what can make people smile—or, after all, make them happy —and that they, on the other hand, know me since they are able to see in me what can make people smile or happy? Their great number, as well as their inability to reach a consensus on this matter beforehand, pleads in their favor; but on the other hand, I see nothing that might support my cause. I am therefore forced to admit that there exists within me something quite visible and objective, something likeable or amusing, which my subjectivity renders invisible to my eyes. Here's yet another piece of evidence to add to the list of this irksome character's liabilities, as if there weren't enough already! Ah! Mordechai Schamz takes to dreaming, if it were only possible to unload oneself entirely on other people, how light life would be! You would only need to go up to the first person passing by and ask him, Am I cheerful, am I sad, is it beautiful, is it good or is it bad? And once the answer is given, you would be on your way, even lighter still, if possible. Considering only the case before me now, am I not, in the eyes of many, the most jolly sort of rake, a genuine public clown? Yes, but it is quite possible that those who do not smile at the sight of me, who are even more numerous, find me a rather glum specimen. So ought I not to be on the alert to change my mood according to whom I meet, not to mention that I would be unable to shirk the demands of individual consciousnesses in quest of their own reality as I am of my own? All things considered, concludes Mordechai Schamz, it is far simpler for me, after all, to subscribe to the feeling of the first person chance sends my way, and which is as valid as any other.

Mordechai Schamz has never forgotten these words of Christ: "I have manifested thy name unto the men which thou gavest me out of the world," this because of the "out of the world." Indeed, he says to himself, every man who is in the world is "out of the world" and yet I, who am a man and in the world, do not find myself there. Being in the world does not place me, as others, out of it, but alongside its outerness. Might it be that I am not a man like others? I do not, however, see what the reason would be since I am, like others, a man and in the world. I would not be like others, indeed, if I were not of the world, but the simple fact that I do not feel myself to be out of it is proof that I am, and even that I can conceive in what manner others are there. Might I therefore be like the others without being there like them? Such is not possible, since it is the place they occupy that makes their very nature, which is also my own. Might I then be like them without feeling so? In actual fact, this explanation is far from satisfying to me, and yet I can choose no other. To be brief, I am out of the world because I can be no other place. I am there, in a certain fashion, against my will. Might I not have put my finger on something here? Mordechai Schamz asks himself. Might it not be quite simply that I do not feel myself to be out of the world because I do not want to be? But why wouldn't I want to be? Because I would like there to be something other in its place? Gladly—but what would I desire to place there if not myself? I would not like to set up another in the place which is my own and falls to me by birth, by nature, and by law! Another, why not, after all, if it is another me? Might I not judge myself worthy to be out of the world and might I be waiting, so as to feel myself there, to have made myself worthy all the while being there nevertheless? If thus it is, my position is comparable to a stylite's on his column, crying out all day long toward heaven: "My God, I am not worthy to be here!"—the difference being, remarks Mordechai Schamz, that he can come down but I cannot.

From Mordechai S. to G.

My Darling,

For I know that you are also my son, and I, who am a bad son, why would I not be to any less an extent a bad father? Perhaps, by better feeling the responsibility I have for you on this earth by being myself, I will become at last aware of what actually is. For if I cannot feel you through the harm that you cannot do me, it is possible on the contrary that I feel you by the harm I do you. Words! words! each time upon writing to you, will I only speak of how vain it is to write you? How wearisome this is for me, who am always wearied. And how wearisome this must be for you, who only are! But let me get back to what I was saying—if I were to know the harm I do you, by bearing you so badly on this earth, obviously I would not do it. But my lot is always the same: to know without knowing. To know, yes, but without knowing I know. It is as if I were a traveler gone astray one foggy night and I were to ask directions of myself, an inhabitant of the region, and this latter would direct me toward an invisible point through the fog. This latter would know the way and would have informed the other of it, who would then also know it, without however either of them seeing it. And here once again we face this twofold invalid, this me and this me—or these two invalids in one, whichever I wish, whichever you wish. Here he is again, the man who shouts: I want to know, I must know—yet who will not know; who knows that whether or not on the day knowledge comes, it will not come to him; who knows that for knowledge to come, he must no longer be. And if he were no longer to want to know? he asks himself at times—then answers himself: Ah, if he were no longer to want, he would no longer be himself. He who can talk to himself is the man who can say everything about himself. He can say that he wants to know while knowing that he cannot—that he wants not to be, while knowing that he cannot. There is nothing that his speech cannot make of him; in such a way has he made himself. But he who can say nothing, who can want nothing, who can know nothing nor make nothing of himself, you alone are the one who made him; it is in you alone that he makes himself.

Mordechai

Mordechai Schamz likes the times in which he lives. You must be a man of your times, he declares, absolutely and without the slightest reservation. As a matter of fact, unless you are a ghost, how could you not be? Every man is of his times, and reflects them, as people say, whether he wants to or not. If I take myself as an example—well now, I don't at all see how I can be the reflection of my times, and even if it made any sense, I wouldn't want to be. And yet I reflect them, like each and every one of us, because where would the times exist if not within those who are living them? Yet, observing them within me I am quite unable to see them such as they appear outside of myself. There can be only one reason for this: either they are not what they seem to be—or I am not what I seem to be. One or the other, in this confrontation, must disappear, and I don't see why, being a de facto judge and referee, I would not declare myself victorious before I have even engaged in battle. Here I am, therefore, alone on stage, the times stretched out flat at my feet, annihilated. For if the times are not what they appear, what, then, can they be? What can the times be if they are not to be found in their appearance, in the actions which make them up, the events which punctuate them? Therefore the times do not exist, except in those who live them and see them within themselves and for themselves. The times, consequently, are in the man, and not the man in the times. So it is not all that surprising, notes Mordechai Schamz, that I like my times because they are wholly within me and belong to me, and when they appear to me outside of myself, I am still the one who is seeing them. Yes—but how does it come about that in such a case they appear to be different from what they are inside of me? Ah, it's because I make them so, he retorts; can it be otherwise? But why then create for myself times for external use when I already have them within myself? Perhaps in order to be able to say that I am living in such times and not that they are living within me. No question, indeed, that to conceive of myself as being the times I live in, I would feel myself simultaneously too alone and too numerous, too silent and too noisy, too motionless and too restless. The worst of all being, observes Mordechai Schamz, that it would be impossible for me to choose which of these two extremes to really be.

Mordechai Schamz ought to pay more attention to himself than he does. Despite his heft and hale and hearty features, he appears so light and fragile! He gives the strange impression that a gust of wind could blow him away, a shift in the weather dissolve him, as if he were a piece of paper, the brief materialization of a fleeting thought. But there are threats far less imaginary hovering over his existence in such great numbers that if he took account of them, he would not budge from his chair. Quite to the contrary, he wants to know nothing of them—their negative character at least, for they have numerous positive sides, which he knows how to exploit and make the most of. Are they not, he remarks, so many proofs that I am, these forces whose aim is that I no longer be? As a matter of fact, if their aim were simply that I no longer be, it is likely their exploit would have succeeded a long while since and so well so that I would never perhaps even have existed. On the contrary, totally crowned with success as far as my past is concerned and held at bay by my vigilance as far as the present goes, their efforts are marked by a definite, repulsive, and invigorating effect; and if I did not feel my rear guard under ceaseless assault, there is no proof I would find in myself the necessary resolution to continue along my path. On the other hand, if they relentlessly labored to erase my tracks, and the man I know myself to be would not do so, it is altogether certain that I would sink a considerable part of the time remaining into contemplating them, an activity as useless as it is fatuous. All things considered, concludes Mordechai Schamz, these forces, by the very fact they are its enemy, are not merely the proof but also the very mainspring of my continuity. However, if it is with reason that I congratulate myself about their action upon a past that their power has doomed to nothingness, I hesitate to draw any deductions from this, regarding any possible effect of such a power upon my present. I know my present, such as it is, but what do I know of what it would be without these forces? Perhaps they snatch from me the major part—fabulously rich, infinite regions—so as to leave me with, as to a book its cover, or to a shipwrecked soul his sufficient and providential plank, nothing but this tiny piece of thought. At any rate, what lingers with me, notes Mordechai Schamz, is the invaluable consolation of knowing that I will never know anything about it.

Mordechai Schamz walks. One stride, then the other, followed by another, etc., in such a way that he moves forward. There is no other activity he prefers to this one. No doubt, it is often utilitarian but even more often it is gratuitous, and that is the way he likes it best. Really, it is a pure satisfaction whose signs can be recognized on his face at the moment he prepares to leave for his stroll. As for this satisfaction, if you were able to continue scrutinizing its clues, you would subsequently see it dwindle a little, for what he prefers is the moment of departure. Isn't each time, he says to himself, like a new birth, this instant when, shoes all laced up, overcoat slipped on, you rise from the chair to dash outdoors? Yes, he continues, I did indeed speak of dashing out, for it is exactly like taking flight, and the outdoors beckons in promise like a sky, like an emptiness. I do not fly, however, and that is all the same to me. Providence gave flight to the birds and walking to men, and if the opposite were to be, well then the opposite would be. Nevertheless, between these two activities, the difference resides only in the place where they are exercised, not in their essence. Birds fly the way men walk and vice versa; it is an obvious fact. All it takes is a little judgment and a spirit of observation to perceive this. Endowed with a little more weight, birds would walk; endowed with a little more lightness, men would fly, and that is all the difference. The lightness man does not have in his body, he has in his mind, and it is by this very quality that it is possible for him to reason such as I am doing. Birds, if they have lightness in their wings, have a heaviness in their tiny heads, and if they cannot admire what seems to plod along under them, it is rather due to this weight. Whereas man admires what flies above his head and even possesses the capacity to envy it at the same time he is able to be satisfied with his state. That is why I am fully entitled to deem myself happy to walk, thinks Mordechai Schamz. For I know what it means to walk and to fly, and by walking I do exactly as a bird that flies, even while not doing so.

Mordechai Schamz remembers. He remembers the cold of winters past, the heat of summers, the beauties of the sky at sunset, fragments of popular songs and melodies. To tell the truth, he particularly likes to remember, and the moments during the day are rare when he does not solicit his memory. Oh, of course he scarcely depends on its fidelity and knows how much his faculty named *memory* owes to an inventiveness whose indications abound. But that matter is, all told, of no importance for what he likes most is to turn his mind on the past, even the very recent past. He is, it might be said, a collector of memories and, as everyone knows, beauty owes nothing to great age. With his memories, he makes edifices of sorts, broad and light, whose elements he inverts and changes at will. His will, in point of fact, so sovereignly dominates their construction and arrangement that he effortlessly manages to remember one and the same event, one and the same period, one and the same instant, with nostalgia or disgust, regret or relief. In this art he manifests such a mastery that he can rightfully compare his excellence to that, for example, of the most eminent poets, and it is with the feeling of not insulting his memory that he happens to evoke fraternally, on the occasion of particular successes, the figure of Basho the monk. Your haiku—thus he addresses him across the ages—are they not brothers of my memories? And were you more able than I to analyze this practice pure as the air by which both one and the other are conceived? Between the world and our gaze, indeed, there is air—what we do not see and yet without which nothing would be such as it is. It changes nothing, whereas without it everything would be changed. Likewise our art is as present and absent as the air, and we will never be able to appreciate its effects upon the things it absorbs more than we do with that of the air upon the universe it bathes. Thus they go along a few moments side by side, Mordechai Schamz and Basho the monk, as if time, by means of a brief eclipse, had placed these two pilgrims on the same road.

As certain accidents of fate would have it, Mordechai Schamz's eyes at times fall upon a painting. He always averts them as rapidly as possible. The reason for this is as simple as strange: he unfailingly experiences the impression that the artist himself is presenting his work to him and expects him to express in return his appreciation. Thus he prefers to manifest a crudeness rather than to exercise an authority, which he deems, at the very least and in any case, illegitimate. This impression, he reflects, is curious, but it is not for all of that unjustified. Why, indeed, he further adds, does a painter paint a painting if not for it to be looked at and appreciated—and by whom if not me in the present case? It is therefore quite as if he were holding it out with both arms toward me, thus displaying, to my mind, an equal thoughtlessness and presumptuousness; for I see nothing which authorizes him to solicit from whomever and at once faculties as precious and intimate as those of attention and judgment. Thus it is not only without any trouble that I refuse him them, but with the feeling of exercising a right which to me is as fundamental as inalienable. It is nevertheless strange, remarks Mordechai Schamz, that I am alone in feeling the thing among the mass of my fellow creatures who go so far as to congregate and even pay in order to see themselves deprived of it. But no doubt it is, on the contrary, for the purpose and the satisfaction of exercising this same right that they act the way they do. Apparently we do not have much of a fellow likeness to each other as it seems, since I deem myself forced where they feel themselves invited, and despoiled where they esteem themselves prodigal. It is not impossible that on this point there is a deficiency or poverty or, more simply, a shyness on my part. Yes, shyness, he says to himself, is perhaps the word; but can a person remake himself? And since, instead of remaking himself, a person prefers to remake the world, he takes to dreaming of one where the works of man would be presented to him as anonymously and spontaneously as are lakes, flowers, villages, and mountains to a stroller's eyes. Thus, he says to himself, our vanity's role would be reduced to nothing, and neither could we determine the role of chance nor of our own will to perform better than chance. Under these conditions, concludes Mordechai Schamz, my shyness—or whatever other name this strange modesty may have—would no longer have any grounds for existing, and in the same way that it would be possible for me to cast upon all things a gaze of equal limpidity, I would also be able to offer this limpidity in my person to all eyes.

At times Mordechai Schamz thinks about future generations. Quite curiously, the reason is to ask himself what they will owe him. Yes, that is quite curious, he remarks, since for them to owe me something I would first need to give them the opportunity, and what I am very certain of is that there will be no mark left of me in my wake. However, is it really necessary that I leave after me these marks that are seen in books and on monuments? There is no cause to doubt that there existed many men who secretly and anonymously influenced the course of history, perhaps even in greater numbers than those whose memory it has preserved. Who knows if, among them, there were not some whose influence was so secret that it remained such even to themselves, and who knows, furthermore, if I do not or will not number among those? Not I, in any case, which does not invalidate—nor by the same token validate—my hypothesis in any way. All the same, remarks Mordechai Schamz, the point here is not speculation, but feeling. Yes, I have the strong feeling that the generations coming after me already owe me something and perhaps, precisely, by the very fact that they will owe me absolutely nothing. I will say, if it is possible to think such a thing, what they owe me is that they are in my debt for nothing. Is not that something, and even a great deal, being able to consider that, among the billions who have preceded us in order to each build his share, however infinitesimal, of the world given us, there is at least one among them, and perhaps only one alone, who has neither built, nor given nothing? Depending on your wishes and whether you view it in a positive or negative light, is it not a consolation, an encouragement, or an example of the most precious kind? Being able, as it were, to raise your head and see—amid this inextricable jumble of efforts and actions—this compact mass of wills and intentions, a blank, a void, swaying, imponderable, like a balloon vanishing very high in the sky, an almost imperceptible rip in the opacity of the clouds, is it not, regardless of how you take it, a kind of joy? Ah, how very unfortunate, notes Mordechai Schamz, that it is impossible for anyone to ever experience it.

Mordechai Schamz likes very much to look into the windows of flower shops. Flowers, naturally, are not something he has at home, but the idea that others buy them and carry them off to be placed in their homes gives him even more pleasure than if he himself were to do it. He experiences a sweet contentment when imagining a bouquet soon-to-be wrapped and transported through the streets, then shorn of its paper and arranged in a vase to be, in the house of men, a bit of nature—nearer, soothing, peaceful. He would be able, strictly speaking, to carry some in his hand, but it never occurred to him to introduce some, even if only one, in his room. He does not know for that matter if it is due to the flower or the room —he only knows that the thing is impossible. However, he reflects, what could possibly happen? Might the flower instantly wither, is it the room that might explode? Undoubtedly nothing of the kind, or even nothing whatsoever would occur—there would be flowers in the room and that is that. And yet, such a thing is impossible. Is it because I might be struck by lightning before having opened the door or that the flower might be taken from me by some invisible agent, one with wings no less? It remains that the thing is impossible all the while being possible, and possible despite the fact it is not. This obstinate confrontation of two worlds of potentiality does not fail to intrigue Mordechai Schamz— this all the more so since he is the site for it. I am not only the site for it, he reflects, but equally so the author, the omnipotent creator. This impossibility, which is a result of my doing, should prove able, therefore, by my doing to be annihilated; and yet it cannot be. Might it then be that it is not a result of my doing? This does not necessarily follow; indeed, that the impossibility results from my doing does not imply that the possibility of the opposite also be the case. In other terms, that I have made impossible the fact that my room be flowered does not mean that I can make possible the fact that it be so. If therefore I believe my reasoning here, I am only responsible for half of the fact that my room cannot be flowered—the impossibility is only half due to the fact of being me. Who, therefore, can be responsible for the other half—the flowers? I would have one chance out of two of discovering this, Mordechai Schamz says to himself, if it were possible for me to move out.

Mordechai Schamz has no imagination. As for what other people's lives are like, he has not the slightest idea. Thus his life is all of life. Ah! sighs he, if I were able to experience only the slightest bit of what the life is of those I brush past each day, I would not be so subject to my own. In the end, am I so? Hardly. If it were a disease, he further adds in the same metaphorical mode, I would have it, naturally, despite not feeling it, as far as I can tell. Therefore might the imagination then be necessary not only to experience the life of others but equally one's own? Might it then be that it is entirely of the imagination? Such is not possible, for in that case I would be without life. And why not? Cannot a person live without life? Certainly yes—I am proof of it: I live, I live a life, my life —apparently I can do no less—but not life. To live life, on the other hand, necessitates, in my opinion, that a person possesses the capacity to project the image of it, to generalize it at the same time as he ramifies it, to extend it so as to all the better reduce it and to fragment it so as to delimit its essence—in short, that a person imagine it. Someone born out at sea on a raft would not know he is shipwrecked, for he would not even have the capacity to imagine that there exist lives that are not those of a shipwrecked man. I, all the same, upon this flat rock in the middle of the torrent, I can only multiply to infinity, if it so amuses me, the image of a man upon a flat rock in the middle of a torrent and those eyes which in the street search me as I search them with a gaze identical to my own. It would be amusing, however, muses Mordechai Schamz, that this knowledge I have of life be exact—that a thing such as the science of life exist and that I be the sole one to possess it. Then, everyone else would be mistaken in imagining their lives through what they imagine about the life of others, and I alone, though not seeing any farther than the tip of my toes, would be right. We would all be as I am upon this flat rock, and it is thus that I would see, as far as my gaze focuses, the whole of humanity enthralled by delusive reveries whose nature I would be alone to recognize. That said, remarks Mordechai Schamz, would I instantly discover that such is the case and that nothing would be changed for all of that? I would still and always be alone with only this life, and in this case I can always just as well decide that I alone in the world have imagination.

Mordechai Schamz has never been able to take anything seriously. He does not even know what that means. In truth, reflects he, what about me can be taken as serious? I suppose it is necessary, in order to take seriously anything whatsoever, to be in a position to keep it serious. To take is nothing; possession is what matters. Why does a monkey, grabbing hold of an emerald, not retain it? Likewise, if fate were to go so far as to propose to me to take something seriously, I would have no more reason to keep it than the monkey the emerald. The man who retains the emerald is the man who knows its value and consequently what use he can make of it because he has the means to compare it to that of other things he has or could have in his possession. But this thing that would be proposed to me to take seriously, there is nothing, among what I possess, to which I can compare the value I could extract from it or the use I would be able to make of it; thus it would be quite naturally, and I would go so far as to say *logically*, that, following the example of the monkey, I would toss back this emerald. There is no doubt, remarks Mordechai Schamz, that I would need to make myself over in order for my system, as does the oyster with the catalyzing grain of sand, to be capable of assimilating what is serious, for it is highly probable that this incapacity was mine at birth as, for others, certain diseases or even, according to Descartes, certain ideas. Who knows, he continues, pursuing his reflection along the path where he had begun to push it, if I do not quite simply belong to a type of man which is, in point of fact, defined by the incapacity to take anything seriously— just as certain people are blond, astigmatic, or lucky? I could be, in that as well, the fruit of the designs of nature, which does nothing without reason. Reason possibly being, in the present case and hypothetically, that there is not in the world a sense of the serious in unlimited quantity and that it is better to deprive certain individuals of it rather than afterwards to have to refuse it to those who might experience the need for it. This supposition, concludes Mordechai Schamz, is not as light as might be thought—indeed, would not a person have every reason to be alarmed at the state of the world if monkeys collected precious stones?

From Mordechai S. to Olympe T.

My Dearest Darling,

Do you know, when I evoke you, what first comes to my heart? It is your gentleness. And yet, have you ever shown any toward me? Do not misunderstand me; I simply mean that circumstances have never required you to display any to me—no more than I to you, for that matter—and at any rate it is not in such places where gentleness shows through that we had relations. Therefore, no gentleness between us. And yet you have had it and you should now have so much that your gentleness overflows your intentions and impregnates everything you manifest. I have given this much thought lately—this as much because of you as in consideration of my present state—and I have arrived at the idea that this gentleness one has or does not have is perhaps in direct relation with the reserves of it one possesses. I would have as much trouble explaining to you what I mean by this word as you would have in understanding me. The reason for this is simple: you have as much as possible—I lack as much as possible, so then it is as if a scorpion set about to explain what water is to a fish. But you are intelligent and I have a few memories. Let us say therefore, in broad terms, that the reserves are what you imagine to be the ensemble of forces, capacities, opportunities, chances, ruses from which you can draw so as to understand, taste, maintain, move forward, and use your life—and life itself. You are at an age when the idea does not even occur to consider the nature of life, its volume or its expanse, for each approaching instant seems to bring as much of life as you already have; I am in a state where each approaching instant demands that one invents life for oneself if one wants to be in a position to accompany it and, while passing, take each and every instant with him. But, you will say to me, how does gentleness enter into any of this? Precisely because it was necessary to pass by way of all of this in order to arrive at gentleness. You see that, instant after instant, I function as you do, for it is possible for me to invent, to construct, to produce what you merely have to use, extract, provoke. Thus we are identical in appearance; you through grace, and I through effort, and we differ but on a single point: gentleness which, because it is, so I think, the natural product of the ensemble of forces that I have evoked, has a brightness, a fragrance, as it were, that is impossible to reproduce. I have entirely exhausted it; you still have it entirely. Use it, use it, my gentle girl, even in the very memory of your poor creature, so poor

Mordechai

Mordechai Schamz likes silence very much, the true kind, the sort that's thickest. Nothing is conceived there, no doubt, but neither is anything lost, and it is for that reason he does not hesitate to see in it an image, reduced but faithful, of the universe such as it can be conceived in its most puri- fied form. It is not erroneous, no, he says to himself, to see within myself, at those moments when the silence around me attains its plenitude, a pure image of man in the center of a pure image of the universe. Indeed, however greatly I train my attention, nothing do I discern there but a vibration so feeble that it may be perceptible only by my imagination; no doubt, it is the echo of sweeping movements in which es- sences intermingle and are interchanged, with no possibility of the least particle in their course being abstracted from or added to the myriad mass of these entities. It is such a great shame that in this silence I myself cannot be included, and subsequently that I escape the law of *nil novi sed nove sub sole*. It is quite by the same stroke indeed that, through the sole action of my thought, I produce noise and newness. For in this silence I conceive thoughts, however tenuous they may be and no matter what they are about. But is it not, after all, Mordechai Schamz suddenly questions himself, a simple habit of language that makes me say that I conceive them, whereas nothing indicates to me that I am doing anything other than noting their appearance in my mind—in fact, watching them pass by, borne along by the universal flux that soon abstracts them from my sight—in such a way that by regarding myself as a simple spectator of the incessant and universal metamorphoses of unalterable essences, it is impossible for me to include myself wholly in this process and to consider at the same time that it is my capacity alone to delude myself about my powers that differentiates me from other species which, for their part, contribute blindly, and consequently with no illusions, to the universal oeuvre. No doubt, if I could not deceive myself, I would act exactly as does sandstone, the forget-me-not, or the ferret—that is, I am acting but, so to speak, rather plainly and simply, in total tranquillity. That is why it does not appear unreasonable to me to affirm that to be a man, in the final analysis, is, above and after all, being able to delude oneself. Fortunately, rejoices Mordechai Schamz, being a man also means not being one completely and thus having the ability to sense the trickery through the holes that exist in humanity.

At times, in the depth of the night, seated on a chair, Mordechai Schamz emits strange sounds. They can be compared neither to the lion's roar nor the tiger's growl nor the scream of the hyena, the tawny owl, or the barn owl, nor to the crow's croak or the snake's hiss. Neither do they recall, from near or far, the pant of strenuous effort, the moan of the wounded, or the gasp of the dying. In short, they have nothing—naturally, to the extent that such a thing is possible

—that is animal or human about them; they are, it might be said, purely Schamzian. In fact, upon close reflection, reflects he, if there is something on this earth that is peculiar to myself, truly it is these sounds, for I have not heard them elsewhere and am unable to say where they come from. How then can I claim, he amends himself, that they are what I have that is most personal if I don't know from where they come since they then cannot come from myself? Or is it, on the contrary, that the mystery of their origin is my guarantee that their source cannot be exterior to me, insofar as what comes to me from the exterior can reach me only by means of knowledge? Is it not strange, he asks himself, that after having used the near totality of time which passed into my power in an attempt to know who I am or am not, I reach the point of telling myself that the only thing that is peculiarly mine perhaps is something not only whose origin but also whose meaning, as well as whose function and purpose, I am unaware of? That is strange, undoubtedly, Mordechai Schamz adds further, but nevertheless not impossible, and even less so incomprehensible. What, indeed, is more shared than knowledge? Is it not the case that all that man knows, or at least what he knows for sure, he knows in common? But what he is unaware of, what in him has not yet been able to take a form that knowledge may apprehend, how could this be shared? Thus it can be put forward with assurance that what we know, we all know in common, whereas what we are unaware of, we are alone, each one of us, in our ignorance. It is therefore possible for me to conclude, concludes Mordechai Schamz, that what I am unaware of is the very thing which authentically and exclusively belongs to my person and that, being unaware on certain nights of what I do to emit these sounds which tell me nothing, I do know in any case and with utter certainty that at least I take pains to be Schamzian.

Mordechai Schamz would very much like to paint. But, even if he would have the capability, he cannot see what he would be able to represent. Obviously, he concedes, it is well known that the subject is not what is important, that all that matters is the fashion in which it is represented; all the same, the moment always arrives when the manner must be decided on as to how the surface of the canvas will be occupied. I do not see myself seized with scruples over soiling a virginity of sorts, interrupting a continuity of sorts, the problem does not lie there, apparently, but—but where then does it lie, he suddenly grows impatient, albeit inwardly, if neither in the choice of support nor of technique, nor in the choice of style, nor of subject, nor in the choice of means? Does it lie perhaps, he asks himself, in that of the final end? No doubt, I would like to paint, but to what final end? To paint for its own sake? I doubt there was ever a painter worthy of the name who has done likewise, and I am one, from this fact alone and for this reason alone, who refuses to paint only to paint. If therefore I go by what I am saying—and I have no reason not to do so—I am a painter without a goal, which comes down to saying without a painting. Then by what right may I declare that I would like to paint if I find no reason to do so and that I am a painter if I have never made a painting? That is strange, notes Mordechai Schamz, and it does not fail to irritate me a little, to the extent that I maintain the idea that I am nonetheless a painter. But might it not be, he asks himself, that an error of sorts has slipped into the exposition I have made to myself of the situation? Of course. I was mistaken when declaring that I am a painter without a painting just because I am a painter without a goal. Indeed it is completely the opposite of what I ought to have said. I have a painting—the one I do not want to do because I do not see the final end of it, this implying and explaining that and vice versa. Thus, concludes Mordechai Schamz, I have the perfect right to declare not only that I would like to paint but furthermore that I am a painter, for when I say that I would like to paint that means that I would like to paint in another way than I am doing, which proves in the same stroke that I am a painter.

One day Mordechai Schamz will be confronted with pain. He knows it, he feels it, he waits for it. Obviously, notes he, upon this large surface plane where I am, and so unobstructed on every side it does not even have a horizon to mark its boundary, I do not see from where it might come. I do not see it, that's a fact, but I know it, which is enough. The plane has sides, what's more, that I am unable to perceive by which it can arrive: the top, the bottom, and the center—that is, the interior. Yes, he reflects, quite possibly it comes, for example, from within, and I have been nurturing it there for a very long time unawares until its hour bursts upon me, as a child between the legs of its mother. But what would she do then—cuckoo? I mean by that, what difference would that make whether it passes from the interior to the exterior? In other terms, does pain change by being perceived by consciousness? No doubt the person who perceives it himself changes, but in what respect is it changed for all of that? In fact, if such a thing changes it, the reason is that it does not exist in itself, but only in the consciousness of the person who perceives it. On the other hand, if it is not altered by the fact of being perceived, it comes down to saying that there is no difference between its latent state and its patent state, and therefore that it does not exist, at least for the person who undergoes it. Thus, concludes Mordechai Schamz, regardless of the way it is taken, it seems that pain does not exist—and if man experiences it, the reason is that he invents it through the sensation he has of it. Yet I do not invent it since I do not feel it, and all I have of it is the idea of its eventuality. But why, he asks himself, might that not precisely be my way of feeling it—that is to say, of inventing it? If certain people like feeling it near them, there surely ought to be others, such as myself, with a preference for feeling it far away, without that making much difference to the extent that, close at hand or in the distance, what alone matters is its existence. Oh! this is rather unfortunate, he recognizes, for I imagined pain active in another way and, I might dare say, otherwise activating than this. I was waiting for flashes, bolts of lightning, something that at the very least consumes, and here I am with this vague expectation. Expectation, have I said? Mordechai Schamz questions himself, but how can I wait expectantly for a thing whose presence is in the very wait for its arrival? Therefore, it means that I am not waiting for it and that by waiting all I have done is mistake my verb—or its direct object.

Mordechai Schamz is on the potty. As often happens, this gives him an opportunity to bring to mind those who are likewise situated. Imagine, he thinks, that there are at least several hundred million of us about the same business at this very moment! and that I am one of them, like an animal in the middle of a herd—and that this is the way things are every time I satisfy one of my natural needs. Yes, one can affirm, really, he goes on, that it is quite as if, on such occasions, we were assembled, gathered together, the way cows are in the evening in their stables, whereas the rest of the time we are scattered about, just as they are, in the meadows. Certainly when man eats, sleeps, and drinks, you know what he is doing, but beyond these concrete and compulsory chores, each man finds himself back in his world once more and utterly alone in doing what he does, like a bird in the air or a beast in the bushes, with the result that, you could even go so far as to propose while awaiting proof to the contrary, that man, each man, can be considered and defined with certainty such as he is—that is to say, as belonging to his species, only to the extent which, and at those times when, he performs the actions and satisfies the needs common to every member whereas, once beyond this common measure, he enters into a category peculiar only to himself. Indeed, I don't see, Mordechai Schamz reassures himself, who will be able to assert, and what's more prove, to me that there exists a definition for what speaking, thinking, working, loving, hoping or taking a walk is that is applicable to each man in particular and to men in general, such as there exists for what feeding oneself is or, in the present instance, for defecating. Thus man, he goes on, can be assimilated to his species in exactly the same way as a cow can be to the bovine species and this by using the same criteria and the same logic; but we wish to use others—which, by the way, a person would not dream of doing as far as cows are concerned—and in consequence immediately enter the realm of pure invention. If therefore I can believe myself in this matter, concludes Mordechai Schamz, following words with action, at the very moment I unstick my buttocks from the oval seat I cease being a man beyond any doubt and can just as well announce I am a butterfly.

Mordechai Schamz's coat reaches down very low, all the way to his feet, entirely covering him up. Only his head sticks out—and then, not all of it, whenever the weather requires that he protect his crown with a hat. So that he appears at such times, to someone's passing glance, as a fragment of a face which might well be borne along by some mechanism underneath. Coincidentally, whenever he pictures himself in general, this is how he most likes to imagine himself: as resembling a short sentence taken out of a long speech. Quite obviously, this applies to what we all show of ourselves but in my case, he thinks, I like dreaming that the essential is here and the rest does not exist. Yet don't I owe it to myself to be honest, he corrects himself, and to frankly admit that beyond liking to have this dream, I do what I can to realize it, even while knowing beforehand my effort is useless? Am I not heading toward the sort of existence wherein my whole being might be captured with a glance, a few words, a quick circle a hand traces in the air? Ah, he exclaims in the silence of his inner self, if it is true that you prepare yourself lifelong for the end of your life, wouldn't it be perfectly delightful to be able at a second's notice, in a summing up which is as swift as it is careless, as complete as it is useless, to assure yourself that this is really where it all is, in this paraphernalia—a head on a coat and under a hat, for example, or the gentle breeze of a vague desire, or the memory of a possible happiness, all on the point of being dashed? A sentence, I was saying, continues Mordechai Schamz, but I would be able to make do with a page, provided that it be very carelessly written and only treated such nebulous realities that they would be ludicrous or soporific or both at the same time, if possible. Since it is a good thing, he goes on, to maintain your desires, even the least reasonable ones, within the limits if not of the realizable, at least of the plausible, I would even go so far as to grant, for the sake of argument, that I could be held in as many pages as I could hold in one hand, so that when the final instant is upon me,

I will hold them in view and I will say, in one final breath, in a parody of satori which will arrive in the nick of time all the same and whose exotic humor will not fail to escape me in the midst of contemplating this totality: So this was Mordechai Schamz.

Mordechai Schamz is not pretentious. In fact, he has never pretended to lay claim to anything. Rather, such attributes are what, if he takes himself at his word, lay claim to him. As far as he is capable of going back in his own time, he has not even the minutest memory of having laid claim to anything whatsoever. On the contrary, he was only able to experience the progressive, continuous appending to his person of the most heterogeneous attributes through a phenomenon comparable in all points to that which attaches metallic objects to a magnet. However, remarks he, the magnet must of course possess an attractive power, and I cannot pretend to claim, on my side, that I am devoid at the very least of a certain capacity to receive and preserve the above-mentioned attributes. I do not see how, indeed, the most minuscule of these parasites could have been able to cling to me if I had rejected it. The reason is that, all told, reflects he, passivity does not suffice; it is a matter, it was a matter, not of undergoing but only of repelling. Thus, I perhaps do not lay claim to the possession of attributes, but I tend toward it at least, which comes down to the same thing, and the fact that this tendency is, in all probability, innate, in no way excuses my error. In this affair, there is really no other than myself I can incriminate; I should have known, I should have wanted. However, how could I have been able to know without previously attributing to myself this knowledge and this will without possessing the will? But I suspect, Mordechai Schamz replies to himself, that once again these are bad excuses, and that examples exist in sufficient quantity to prove to me the validity of my suspicions. Let us begin over again. How does the magnet go about transforming itself into a rusty hedgehog? It is certainly not by staying in its box. Likewise, if I were not to have let myself be dragged along by this unfortunate mind of a collector to wherever it had a whim to go, I would not be reduced to bearing its weight—nor the noise of all this clattering hardware I find myself loaded down with. Still, Mordechai Schamz consoles himself, nothing is lost yet. Every magnet attracts. I'll surely find a way to invent one for myself, and if I have been able all this time to pretend I know and have the ability without reality ever disabusing me, I still have at least as much time, and as much chance, to pretend I have forgotten.

It would please Mordechai Schamz to be kind. It is not that he lacks kindness—what he lacks is an object to which he can be made to feel it. Without an object, indeed, notes he, how can kindness manifest itself? However, a fact as mysterious as strange, I feel myself kind. The thing is mysterious indeed, for I have nothing to measure it against and I thus find myself in the position of a man plunged in the most perfect darkness who is persuaded that his sight is not at fault. But perhaps, all told, kindness is one of those things that cannot be measured by the ell of reality. It is possible that I possess kindness in its pure state, as it were, the way you have a liver and arteries whose functioning you do not need to feel in order to be assured that you possess them. It is even possible, he goes on further, that the scant concern I display about the proofs of its existence are the very measure of its quality—or of its quantity, however you please—and that inversely those who accumulate its manifestations do nothing but make evident their anxiousness as to its presence in their person. Oh, confesses Mordechai Schamz, the thing would be amusing if it were verified. But is it not already so at least in part? What does a person do, if you consider the matter a moment, who displays kindness? He does nothing, truly, but project it upon an object which, by the effect kindness has upon it, reflects back its image, using this object as a mirror, as it were, to return it to himself. So that the person who, in the final judgment, feels it is he who has displayed it. It is therefore to his advantage, after all, that he exercises it and the fact that opinion gauges the kindness of a man exactly in function of the negligence he shows when choosing the objects for his kind deeds is, so it strikes me, a proof that we would be hard put to refute. Despite everything, concludes Mordechai Schamz, all the better if we are mistaken on this point, and so much more the better for whosoever is equally mistaken; regardless, I will not be left with any less kindness to dispense to the air or the desert, whichever you wish, and that falls, like drops of dew, upon the desert in the morning.

Of course, there is many a moment when Mordechai Schamz thinks it would be pleasant to change. But what can he do, he who is given over wholly to time, other than to go along with it? And has anyone ever seen time change? It would at least be necessary, he muses, that time form a knot in which I would be caught, and my course halted or else that it have a hiccup which unseats me, leaving me on the edge of its stream, like a thrown rider upon the edge of a road. I would then be at utter leisure to observe myself from head to toe and to meditate upon the changes to be operated upon this interesting subject. However, for the sake of honesty, I must recognize that, no longer being in time, I will be able to be only in eternity, where the present state of my information does not permit me to suppose that you can do anything, for I know at least this with certainty, that action, or in any case the changes resulting from it, cannot be separated from time. Thus I would perhaps be able to act, strictly speaking, but it is obvious that this action would not be followed by any result. But, Mordechai Schamz suddenly questions himself, is not my present state what I am quite exactly in the act of describing? So it is, and very precisely, down to the last comma and least sigh. Indeed, no doubt I act, for there is no way to do otherwise, but without my actions generating the slightest change. Might it then be that I find myself not in time but already in eternity? This "already" is redundant for, after all, time is merely the means we dispose of to experience eternity. Might it then be possible that, all the while experiencing it in the only manner at my disposal, through time, I nevertheless behave, unawares, as if I knew that I am there? So that it would be my acute consciousness of time that paralyzes me, which causes me to live there as if I were not there. But that is absurd, for being in time is being to the same degree in eternity—there is no way for a man to avoid one or the other, whatever consciousness he may have of anything whatsoever. It is not a creature of flesh, but only one of thought that can exist on earth without being present there and be present there without existing. Should I therefore, Mordechai Schamz questions himself, thus conclude that this is what I am?

From Mordechai S. to G.

My Adored One,

   I lately thought about something: these letters I pretend to
address to you, what if you pretended not to receive them?
For, after all, between us, everything belongs to the realm of
pretense. Please understand me, I do indeed say between
us—in other terms, it is our exchange which belongs to the
realm of pretense, not what we are in relation to each other,
through each other, each in and for the other. But that, for
me, is essentially unknowable and only what can be ex-
changed can be known to me. Thus do I need to simulate an
exchange of sorts, to produce something which may be
exchangeable so as to procure myself, from what actually
exists and in consequence is unknowable, a knowledge
which, despite and because of the fact it is simulated, is the
only sort I can possess. For your part, it is by the same token
only through simulation that you can make yourself known
by me, since simulation is my only means of acquiring a
knowledge of you. This is the reason I insist that, just as I
pretend to address letters to you, you must pretend, in my
manner, to have a knowledge of them—for the knowledge
you have of them is something I myself cannot conceive.
Thus, it is by this game and this game alone that I can preserve
in myself some notion of you. However, the apprehension
has suddenly come upon me that, wearied at last of me being
satisfied with so little of you, you at last decide that the
moment has come when I ought to learn to desire you yourself, such as I would want to be satisfied only by you. Thus
you would need to withdraw from our simulacrum and I
would remain there alone, utterly without you. That would
be good, no doubt, if I were to have a means of knowing it,
but how would I perceive that you have withdrawn from this

game I am conducting and which is mine alone? I would be without you, unawares, and it would be a far worse misfortune than if I were to know it, for I would not be able to feel it. Here is why I beg you, Beloved, to leave me in the sorrow of being unaware of your presence, for it is alone by the sorrow of this unawareness that I know you, whereas the sorrow of being unaware of your absence would be the satisfaction I have gone through so much trouble to forget, in which I would be lost.

Mordechai

DALKEY ARCHIVE PAPERBACKS

PIERRE ALBERT-BIROT, *Grabinoulor.*
YUZ ALESHKOVSKY, *Kangaroo.*
FELIPE ALFAU, *Chromos.*
 Locos.
 Sentimental Songs.
ALAN ANSEN,
 Contact Highs: Selected Poems 1957-1987.
DJUNA BARNES, *Ladies Almanack.*
 Ryder.
JOHN BARTH, *LETTERS.*
 Sabbatical.
AUGUSTO ROA BASTOS, *I the Supreme.*
ANDREI BITOV, *Pushkin House.*
ROGER BOYLAN, *Killoyle.*
CHRISTINE BROOKE-ROSE, *Amalgamemnon.*
GERALD BURNS, *Shorter Poems.*
GABRIELLE BURTON, *Heartbreak Hotel.*
MICHEL BUTOR,
 Portrait of the Artist as a Young Ape.
JULIETA CAMPOS,
 The Fear of Losing Eurydice.
ANNE CARSON, *Eros the Bittersweet.*
LOUIS-FERDINAND CÉLINE, *Castle to Castle.*
 London Bridge.
 North.
 Rigadoon.
HUGO CHARTERIS, *The Tide Is Right.*
JEROME CHARYN, *The Tar Baby.*
MARC CHOLODENKO, *Mordecai Schamz.*
EMILY HOLMES COLEMAN,
 The Shutter of Snow.
ROBERT COOVER, *A Night at the Movies.*
STANLEY CRAWFORD,
 Some Instructions to My Wife.
RENÉ CREVEL, *Putting My Foot in It.*
RALPH CUSACK, *Cadenza.*
SUSAN DAITCH, *Storytown.*
PETER DIMOCK,
 A Short Rhetoric for Leaving the Family.
COLEMAN DOWELL, *The Houses of Children.*
 Island People.
 Too Much Flesh and Jabez.
RIKKI DUCORNET, *The Complete Butcher's Tales.*
 The Fountains of Neptune.
 The Jade Cabinet.
 Phosphor in Dreamland.
 The Stain.
WILLIAM EASTLAKE, *Castle Keep.*
 Lyric of the Circle Heart.
STANLEY ELKIN, *Boswell: A Modern Comedy.*
 Criers and Kibitzers, Kibitzers and Criers.

 The Dick Gibson Show.
 The MacGuffin.
 The Magic Kingdom.
ANNIE ERNAUX, *Cleaned Out.*
LAUREN FAIRBANKS, *Muzzle Thyself.*
 Sister Carrie.
LESLIE A. FIEDLER,
 Love and Death in the American Novel.
RONALD FIRBANK, *Complete Short Stories.*
FORD MADOX FORD, *The March of Literature.*
JANICE GALLOWAY, *Foreign Parts.*
 The Trick Is to Keep Breathing.
WILLIAM H. GASS, *The Tunnel.*
 Willie Masters' Lonesome Wife.
ETIENNE GILSON, *The Arts of the Beautiful.*
C. S. GISCOMBE, *Giscome Road.*
 Here.
KAREN ELIZABETH GORDON, *The Red Shoes.*
PATRICK GRAINVILLE, *The Cave of Heaven.*
GEOFFREY GREEN, ET AL., *The Vineland Papers.*
HENRY GREEN, *Concluding.*
 Nothing.
JIŘÍ GRUŠA, *The Questionnaire.*
JOHN HAWKES, *Whistlejacket.*
ALDOUS HUXLEY, *Antic Hay.*
 Point Counter Point.
 Those Barren Leaves.
 Time Must Have a Stop.
GERT JONKE, *Geometric Regional Novel.*
TADEUSZ KONWICKI, *A Minor Apocalypse.*
 The Polish Complex.
ELAINE KRAF, *The Princess of 72nd Street.*
EWA KURYLUK, *Century 21.*
DEBORAH LEVY, *Billy and Girl.*
JOSÉ LEZAMA LIMA, *Paradiso.*
OSMAN LINS, *The Queen of the Prisons of Greece.*
ALF MAC LOCHLAINN,
 The Corpus in the Library.
 Out of Focus.
D. KEITH MANO, *Take Five.*
BEN MARCUS, *The Age of Wire and String.*
WALLACE MARKFIELD, *Teitlebaum's Window.*
 To an Early Grave.
DAVID MARKSON, *Collected Poems.*
 Reader's Block.
 Springer's Progress.
 Wittgenstein's Mistress.
CARL R. MARTIN, *Genii Over Salzburg.*
CAROLE MASO, *AVA.*
HARRY MATHEWS, *Cigarettes.*
 The Conversions.

Visit our website: www.dalkeyarchive.com

DALKEY ARCHIVE PAPERBACKS

Visit our website: www.dalkeyarchive.com